W9-BTM-432

big NATE

ALL WORK AND NO PLAY

More

big NATE

adventures from

LINCOLN PEIRCE

big NATE
ALL WORK AND NO PLAY

A COLLECTION OF SUNDAYS

by LINCOLN PEIRCE

Andrews McMeel
Publishing, LLC

Kansas City • Sydney • London

Andrews McMeel Publishing, LLC
an Andrews McMeel Universal company
1130 Walnut Street, Kansas City, Missouri 64106

www.andrewsmcmeel.com

12 13 14 15 16 SHO 10 9 8 7 6 5 4 3

ISBN: 978-1-4494-2567-8

Library of Congress Control Number: 2012936727

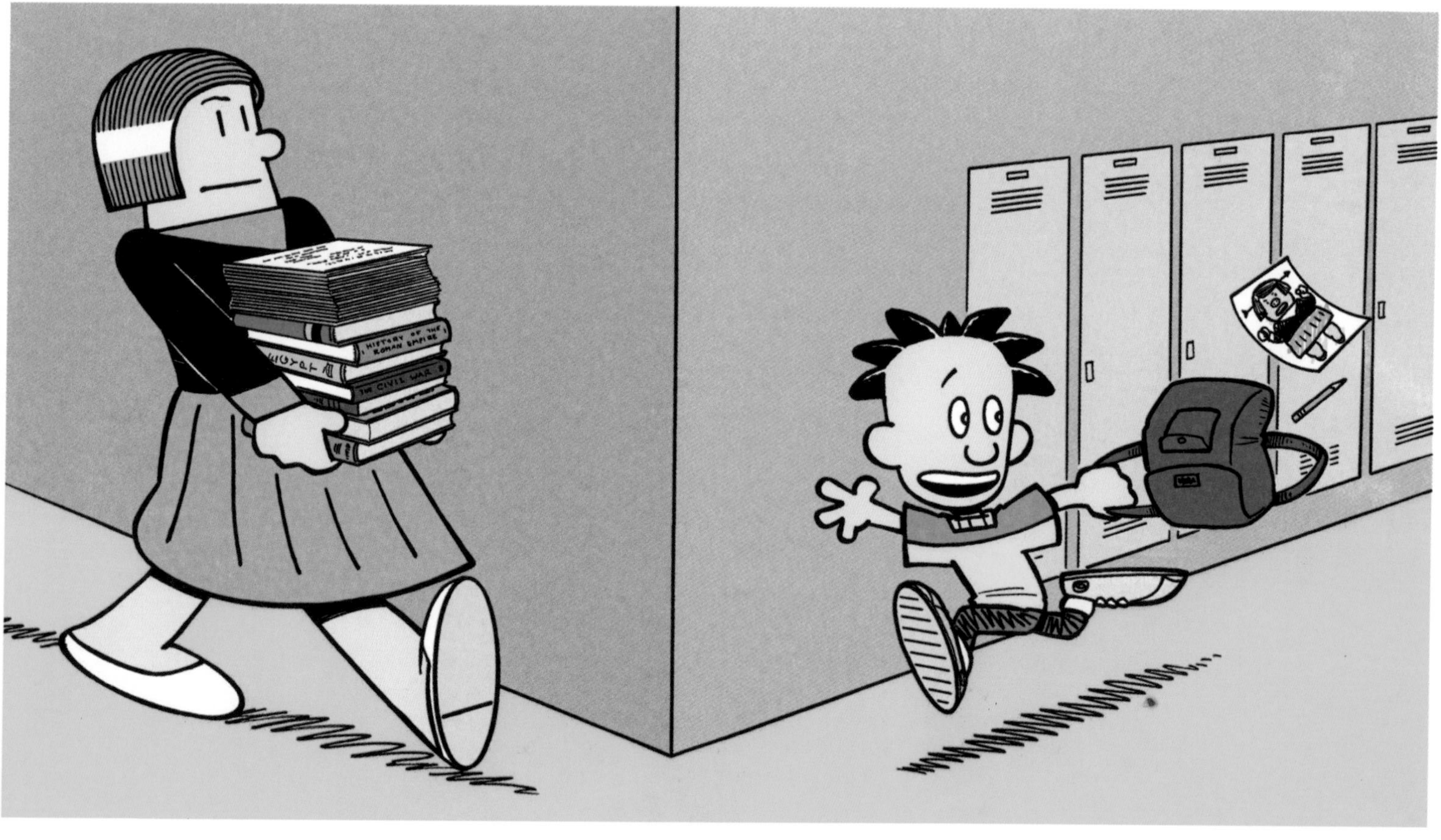

HISTORY OF THE ROMAN EMPIRE
EGYPT
THE CIVIL WAR

MAN! IT'S **POURING** OUT THERE!

DANG! WE CAN'T SHOOT HOOPS IN **THIS**!

BUT HERE'S SOMETHING WE **CAN** DO!

WE CAN LOOK AT MY WORLD-FAMOUS "CHEEZ DOODLE" COLLECTION!

LET'S START WITH THIS ONE! IT'S PERFECTLY STRAIGHT INSTEAD OF CURVED! PRETTY UNUSUAL, EH?

...OR HOW ABOUT **THIS**! **FIVE** DOODLES, MAGIC-ALLY LINKED TOGETHER IN A CHEESY, CRUNCHY CHAIN!

HERE'S SOMETHING YOU DON'T SEE EVERY DAY! A DOODLE WITH A **HOLE** IN IT! I ALMOST FAINTED WHEN I SAW **THIS**!

※CHUCKLE!※ THIS ONE'S FUNNY! IT'S SHAPED LIKE THE HEAD OF ABE LINCOLN! UNCANNY, HUH?

NOW, IF CHEEZ DOODLES COULD TALK, THIS **NEXT** ONE WOULD HAVE QUITE A STORY TO—

?

BIG NATE

by Lincoln Peirce

HMM HMM HMM ♪

OH!... DADDY! WILL YOU LET ME KNOW WHEN GORDIE GETS HERE?

HE'S ALREADY HERE, HON.

HE IS?

I'VE BEEN CALLING YOU! GORDIE'S DOWNSTAIRS!

BY HIMSELF? DAAAAAAD! GO KEEP HIM COMPANY!

OH, HE'S NOT BY HIMSELF! NATE'S DOWN THERE WITH HIM!

I THINK THEY'RE LOOKING AT PHOTOS!

!

NAAAAAAATE!

UH... I THINK YOUR SISTER WANTS YOU.

YEAH, YEAH. NOW THIS IS ELLEN DURING HER UNFORTUNATE "PUDGY" PHASE...

...TWO...

by Lincoln Peirce

Time Once Again For The Continuing Adventures OF.....

SUPERDAD!

Simply put, SUPERDAD isn't like other, better-known superheroes!

He's not **FAST**!

Hello? HELLO?

Dang! They hung up!

He's not **STRONG**!

MAN, this remote is heavy!

He's.... well... LOOK at him!

"Apply Rogaine To Affected Area"...

But he **IS** a superhero! Which means when someone is in need... **HE RESPONDS!**

Time to change into my **SUPERDAD** costume!

Yes, he **RESPONDS!**

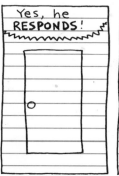

I said... he **RESPONDS!**

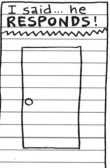

Uh... hello?

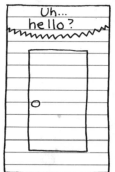

ANY DAY NOW, DAD.

FITTING ROOM 3

✳OOF!✳ SOMETHING'S WRONG!... THIS **CAN'T** BE A 34-INCH WAIST!

SALE

BIG NATE
by Lincoln Peirce

Sir? You'll have to buy those pants.
SALE

WHATCHA DOIN', SON?
DRAWING COMICS.

WHAT KIND OF COMICS?
I DUNNO. JUST COMICS.

FUNNY COMICS? OR ACTION COMICS?
OH.... BOTH, SORT OF.

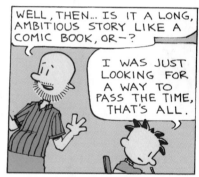
WELL, THEN... IS IT A LONG, AMBITIOUS STORY LIKE A COMIC BOOK, OR—?
I WAS JUST LOOKING FOR A WAY TO PASS THE TIME, THAT'S ALL.

ARE YOU MAKING UP SOME NEW CHARACTERS?
NO, NO... IT'S NOTHING SPECIAL.

IT'S JUST A COMIC! A REGULAR COMIC, JUST LIKE I DRAW EVERY DAY!

"DAD'S REAL LIFE COMICS! EPISODE 6: A HUMILIATING INCIDENT IN A DRESSING ROOM AT THE GAP."
SEE? SAME OLD SAME OLD.

BIG NATE by Lincoln Peirce

The LAST Summer Blockbuster... EVER!!

DAY OF RECKONING!

starring: MOE MENTUM!

Washington, August 1998:

WHAT?? A giant asteroid is on a collision course with Earth?

Right, Mr. President! Only ONE MAN can save us!...

SLADE McSUEDE, soldier of fortune!

Give me a plane, a jackknife, and a box of baking soda, and I'll stop that asteroid COLD!

AND SOON...

Houston, this is McSuede. I'm about to blow this asteroid to kingdom come!

Roger, McSuede!

USA

?!?! oh, NO! My missiles aren't firing!

Backup systems have failed!

DO something, McSuede!

TOO LATE! The asteroid is entering Earth's atmosphere!

THE EARTH IS DOOM

AAAAAH! I SMUDGED!

OH, IT'S NOT THE END OF THE WORLD.

BIG NATE

by Lincoln Peirce

RRRRRINNNNGGG

★☆★☆★☆★☆★☆★

BACK-to-SCHOOL

HIP - HOP!

with master rapper:

"FLUFF DADDY"!

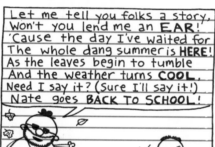

Let me tell you folks a story,
Won't you lend me an **EAR**!
'Cause the day I've waited for
The whole dang summer is **HERE**!
As the leaves begin to tumble
And the weather turns **COOL**,
Need I say it? (Sure I'll say it!)
Nate goes **BACK TO SCHOOL**!

It's a day I get to party but it makes Nate **PANIC**!
It reminds me, just a little, of that flick "**TITANIC**"!
During summer, Nate was sailing on a luxury **SHIP**
But today he'll hit an iceberg with a kung-fu **GRIP**!

CRACK!

Mrs. Godfrey is the reason
For his feelings of dread,
'Cause the woman feasts on students
(And she's very well-fed).
How do **I** feel that my son
Has such a teacher as she?
Let me put it to you this way:
Better **HIM** than **ME**!

While he's dealing with a woman
Who's a sociopath,
I'll be watching "Jerry Springer"
As I lounge in the bath!
While he's doing all the work,
"Fluff Dad" will do all the play!
While he's toiling in the classroom, **I** will...

HAVE A
GREAT DAY!

13

BIG NATE
by Lincoln Peirce

FIELD GOAL!

BOOT!

HUDDLE UP!

HUDDLE UP!

YOU WANNA START OFF AS RECEIVER OR QB?

I'LL BE QB!

OKAY, I'LL GO OUT! I'LL RUN FIVE STEPS UP THE LEFT SIDELINE...

...THEN I'LL ZIG TO THE INSIDE, ZAG TO THE OUTSIDE, THEN...

TEDDY! TEDDY!

YOU'RE GETTING TOO **COMPLICATED**! LOOK WHO'S PLAYING DEFENSE! YOU DON'T EVEN **NEED** A PATTERN!

THIS GUY'S **PATHETIC**! IF YOU JUST RUN IN A STRAIGHT LINE, YOU'LL BLOW RIGHT BY HIM!

I CAN HEAR YOU!!

EITHER THAT, OR HE'LL FALL DOWN!

BIG NATE

by Lincoln Peirce

HIKE!

OOP!

PSST! GUYS! TIMEOUT!

WHAT IS IT?

GROUP OF CUTE GIRLS AT TWELVE O'CLOCK!

OOOOH! **REAL** CUTE!

MAJOR CHANCE TO IMPRESS THE LADIES!

TIME TO SHOW SOME SKIN!

I'LL RUN A POST PATTERN AND MAKE A SPECTACULAR GRAB!

WHOA! WE'RE **ALL** PLAYING! WHY SHOULD **YOU** BE THE ONLY ONE THEY NOTICE?

BECAUSE I'M THE BEST PLAYER, FOOL!

HEY, I'M A **MUCH** BETTER RECEIV-ER THAN **YOU** ARE! JUST GIVE ME THE...

...BALL.

big NATE

by Lincoln Peirce

Panel 1:

Time For Another Edition Of...
CELEBRITY INTERVIEW!
With your host: *Chip Chipson*

Today's Guest: Celebrity Psychic **CLAIRE VOYANT!**

Panel 2:

Greetings, Friends! Today psychic **CLAIRE VOYANT** will make some **PREDICTIONS** about the coming school year!

I knew you were going to say that.

Panel 3:

Claire, what's in the future for everyone's favorite 6th-grade Renaissance Man, **NATE WRIGHT**?

Hmm...

Panel 4:

Nate will be lucky in love. He will be awash in a virtual "babe tsunami."

animal magnetism

Panel 5:

His prodigious athletic skills will bring him great success on the playing field.

Look! NATE'S playing goal!

Why even try?

We forfeit.

Panel 6:

But...hmm...in Nate's **IMMEDIATE** future, something else is coming into focus!... a NUMBER!

Panel 7:

What kind of number, Claire?

Still hazy... It... it's a two-digit number! A **LOW** two-digit number!

Panel 8:

A **12**?

FOR THE NEXT TEST, AT LEAST **PRETEND** TO STUDY.

BIG NATE by Lincoln Peirce

"HI, KATHY!"

"HI, NATE!"

"COVERING THE GAME FOR THE SCHOOL PAPER?"

"YUP!"

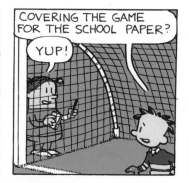

"MAKE SURE YOU PUT SOME GOOD STUFF ABOUT **ME** IN YOUR ARTICLE!"

"AFTER ALL...AS GOALIE, I'M THE **BACKBONE** OF THE TEAM!"

"I'M THE LAST LINE OF DEFENSE!...THE ANCHOR!... THE **ROCK**!"

"HEY, MAYBE YOU COULD EVEN PUT ME IN THE **HEADLINE**!!"

"I CAN ALMOST GUARANTEE IT."

"OOH! HEAR THAT, GUYS? I'M A CELEBRITY!"

BIG NATE

by Lincoln Peirce

Panel 1:
YOU KNOW WHAT'S FUN? STIRRING UP CONTROVERSY AMONG THE FACULTY!

DETENTION

Panel 2:
※ AHEM! ※ HI, MRS. CZERWICKI!

SIT DOWN, NATE.

Panel 3:
YOU KNOW, MRS. CZERWICKI, I WAS JUST THINKING ABOUT YOUR ROLE AS DETENTION MONITOR... IT JUST DOESN'T SEEM FAIR!

Panel 4:
IT'S THE **CLASSROOM** TEACHERS WHO HAND OUT THE DETENTIONS! BUT **YOU'RE** THE ONE LEFT SITTING HERE AFTER SCHOOL!

Panel 5:
THE TEACHERS DROP **THEIR** PROBLEMS IN **YOUR** LAP! I, FOR ONE, AM **OUTRAGED** AT THE WAY THEY TAKE ADVANTAGE OF YOU!

Panel 6:
YOU KNOW, NATE, YOU HAVE A POINT.

Panel 7:
PERHAPS INSTEAD OF SITTING HERE WITH ME, YOU SHOULD BE SPENDING TIME WITH THE TEACHER WHO SENT YOU HERE.

Panel 8:
SOUNDS LIKE SOME SORT OF PARTY IN THE DETENTION ROOM.

DETENTION

BIG NATE

by Lincoln Peirce

Panel 1:

Time Once Again For...

"FEELINGS"

with your host: DR. WARREN FUZZY!

Greetings, soul travelers!

Panel 2:

Friends, I'm here today to talk about a common but serious condition among middle-aged men: "PETER PAN SYNDROME"!

Panel 3:

Peter Pan, of course, is the beloved hero of children's literature who simply REFUSES to grow up!

Panel 4:

Likewise, the world is FULL of men who are determined NOT to act their age!

examples: comb-over   trophy wife

Panel 5:

Desperate to recapture their youth, they feebly attempt to act like the boys they once were, unaware of just how PATHETIC they look!

Word up, homeys!

Panel 6:

How can we help these poor souls? The answer is surprisingly simple: by doing NOTHING!!!

Panel 7:

These men CAN'T turn back Time! Eventually, reality will set in and they'll discover the cruel truth: they're OLD!

Panel 8:

¾GASP!¾... WHEEZE... G-GOING... INSIDE...

FINALLY.

by Lincoln Peirce

HEAR ME, DEMONS OF DARKNESS!

RRRRIINNNNGGG

THERE'S THE BELL! DAY OVER!

TIME FOR OUR FIRST CARTOONING CLUB MEETING OF THE YEAR!

YESSS! THE ONE PART OF SCHOOL I LOOKED FORWARD TO ALL SUMMER!

I MUST SAY, WE HAVE THE BEST CLUB IN SCHOOL! BY **FAR**!

HEY, WAIT'LL YOU SEE THE COMIC STRIP I'M GONNA DRAW ABOUT MRS. GODFREY!

HEE HEE! I'VE GOT A FEW PLANS FOR HER MYSELF!

BOYS! HANG ON A SEC!

HI, MR. ROSA! ON YOUR WAY TO THE CARTOONING CLUB?

NOT TODAY, I'M AFRAID! I'VE GOT A DENTIST APPOINTMENT I'VE ALREADY RESCHEDULED THREE TIMES!

BUT THE CLUB CAN STILL MEET! I ASKED ANOTHER TEACHER TO FILL IN FOR ME AS YOUR ADVISOR! OKAY?

OKAY! THANKS!

HELLO, BOYS.

OH, HOW I HATE HER.

22

WISDOM

WELCOME TO PEER COUNSELING, GUYS! WHAT'S THE PROBLEM?

WELL, I DID THIS DRAWING DURING STUDY HALL...

IT WASN'T JUST **YOU**! WE **BOTH** WORKED ON IT!

IT'S **MY** DRAW-ING! ALL YOU DID WAS THE HANDS AND HELMET!

THAT'S A **LOT**! IT'S **MY** DRAW-ING, **TOO**!

GUYS, **GUYS**! LET'S GET THIS RESOLVED! GIVE ME THE DRAWING AND SIT DOWN!

THIS IS WHAT ALL THE FUSS IS ABOUT? ⁑SMIRK!⁑ NO OFFENSE, GUYS, BUT THIS ISN'T EXACTLY A PICASSO!

WELL, ANYWAY... THERE'S ONLY ONE WAY TO DETERMINE WHO OWNS THIS DRAWING!

WE DIVIDE IT IN **HALF**!

RRR-RIP!

WHAT'S THE MESSAGE HERE, YOU ASK? **COOPERATE** WITH EACH OTHER! **SHARE** EXPERIENCES! **WORK TOGETHER**!

WANNA HAVE A TURN?

HEY, THANKS!

BIG NATE by Lincoln Peirce

LASSIE

SPITSY

ALL RIGHT, SPITSY, LET'S GO FOR A WALK!

HOLD **STILL**, WILL YOU? LET ME GET THIS LEASH ON!

WHOA! SPITSY! STOP! DOWN, BOY! HEEL!!

DANG, SPITSY! YOU ALMOST RIPPED MY **ARM** OFF! COOL YOUR JETS, WILL Y—

YANK!

OKAY, OKAY! I'LL LET YOU RUN FREE! BUT DON'T DO ANY—

ZOOM!

BANG! CRASH!

SPITSY!... **NO!** THAT'S SOMEBODY'S **GARBAGE!**

CHOMPF! SLUP!

LET'S GET OUT OF HERE BEFORE ANY—

!

BAD, BAD, BAD, BAD, BAD, BAD, BAD, BAD, BAD, BAD, BAD, BAD, BAD, BAD, BAD DOG.

GODFREY

big NATE
by Lincoln Peirce

HIKE!

WRIGHT

MUNCH
MUNCH
MUNCH

SLAM!

PERHAPS YOU MISUNDERSTOOD ME WHEN I SAID "GO LONG."

I DIDN'T WANT TO PLAY ANYMORE.

MR. ROSA! CAN WE EAT LUNCH IN HERE?

SURE, GUYS!

IT'S NICE TO BE THE SORT OF TEACHER KIDS FEEL **COMFORTABLE** WITH!

THERE AREN'T MANY CLASSROOMS THEY ACTUALLY **WANT** TO HANG OUT IN!

YAK! YAK!

OF COURSE, NOT MANY TEACHERS ARE AS WELL-LIKED BY THE STUDENTS AS I AM!

THEN AGAIN, YOU'VE GOT TO BE CAREFUL THEY DON'T LIKE YOU **TOO** MUCH!

CHATTER CHATTER BLAH BLAH

YOU CAN'T LET STUDENTS FORGET WHO'S BOSS!

I'LL JUST GIVE THEM A FIRM REMINDER...

YAK YAK YAK

⁑AHEM!⁑ BOYS, QUIET DOWN OR I'LL HAVE TO ASK YOU TO LEAVE.

WA HA HA HA HA HA HA HA HA HA H

...BEFORE IT'S TOO LATE.

HEE HEE! OH, MAN!

GOOD ONE, KEN! CAN I CALL YOU KEN?

BIG NATE

by Lincoln Peirce

Hello, friends! CHIP CHIPSON here with a special report:

AT HOME WITH MRS. GODFREY!!

Mrs. G., a lot of people are wondering: what's your life like AWAY from the class-room? Will you show us around?

Sure, Chip.

E-GAD! A jar of slugs and maggots!

Careful, you fool! That's my dinner!

Nice... um... coffin.

I need a firm mattress.

here?

WAP!

$\frac{17}{102} = \frac{x}{36}$

$12 \times \frac{5}{6} = 120$

$\frac{17}{102} = \frac{x}{36}$

WELL, NATE, I'M GLAD TO SEE YOU WORKING SO HARD.

UNFORTUNATELY YOU'RE WORKING ON **MATH**. THIS IS **SOCIAL STUDIES**.

I WHIPPED OUT THE WRONG DECOY SHEET.

ARE THOSE **DRAWINGS** UNDER THERE?

by Lincoln Peirce

A BANANA PEEL?

YUP! I'VE GOT A POINT TO PROVE!

HAVE YOU EVER SEEN— **REALLY** SEEN—SOMEONE SLIP ON A BANANA PEEL?

WELL, IN CARTOONS I'VE—

AH-**HA!** IN CAR-**TOONS!** BUT NOT IN REAL LIFE!

...AND WHY NOT? BECAUSE BANANA PEELS ARE **NOT** SLIPPERY!

SEE? I COULDN'T SLIP ON THIS IF I **TRIED!**

HMM! YOU'RE RIGHT!

ANOTHER EXAMPLE OF PEOPLE BE-LIEVING A **MYTH!**

PEOPLE JUST DON'T SLIP ON BANANA PEELS IN REAL LIFE! IT **DOESN'T HAPPEN!**

ZZUP!

THIS ISN'T HAPPEN-ING.

PRINCIPAL

SHUT UP

BIG NATE

by Lincoln Peirce

HELLO, friends! BIFF BIFFWELL here! Time for our annual conversation with **HOWARD PLOTZ**, resolution accountant!

Yo, Biff.

As we all know, **HOWARD** here keeps track of all the New Year's Resolutions that people make at this time of year!

Correct

Tell me, Howard. Do people get in trouble when they break a resolution?

Not always, Biff

Some resolutions simply **CAN'T** be kept! They're **MADE** to be broken!

And why's that?

Because they're made under **DURESS!** Usually at the suggestion of a misguided **PARENT!**

What ends up happening? People make resolutions they really **DON'T WANT** to keep!

So... it's **OKAY** to break those kinds of resolutions?

ABSOLUTELY, Biff! To do otherwise would be **UNNATURAL!**

I GOTTA BE ME!

PITY.

Hello, Folks! My name's **KEN DOLITTLE!** Welcome to... **THIS IS YOUR LIFE!**

CLAP! CLAP! CLAP! CLAP!

...And our special guest today is... **DAD!** Guess what, Dad? **THIS IS YOUR LIFE!**

What's a life?

Dad, we've searched the country for friends and neighbors from your past!...People who want to tell you just how much you've **MEANT** to them over the years!

And now it's time to **MEET** those friends and neighbors! Let's bring 'em in, Johnny!

Uh... Johnny?

Yeah, Ken?

ON THE AIR

Where are the friends from Dad's past?

We couldn't find any, Ken.

WHAT ARE YOU WORKING ON?

!

THIS IS MY LIFE.

30

BiG NATE

by Lincoln Peirce

WHAT WAS THE "MAGNA CARTA"? WHO CAN TELL US?

NATE?

ME? BUT I DIDN'T EVEN HAVE MY HAND UP!

YES, I KNOW.

BY SLUMPING DOWN BEHIND YOUR DESK TO AVOID BEING CALLED ON, YOU ACTUALLY DREW **MORE** ATTENTION TO YOURSELF.

THINK ABOUT IT.

WHO CAN TELL US SOMETHING ABOUT THE "STAMP ACT"?

NATE?

ME?

DID YOU OR DID YOU NOT HAVE YOUR HAND UP?

PSST! YOU'RE SLUMPING AGAIN.

NO, I'M JUST BEATEN DOWN...

BIG NATE by Lincoln Peirce

OW.

CARTOON-ING CLUB Meeting TODAY! ROOM 215

GANG, AS YOUR FACULTY ADVISOR, I WANT TO AD-DRESS SOME CON-CERNS ABOUT YOUR CARTOONS.

I'VE NOTICED THAT MANY OF YOU SPEND A LOT OF TIME DRAW-ING CARTOONS ABOUT YOUR CLASSMATES.

THE PROBLEM IS THAT THESE CARTOONS ARE OFTEN CRUEL!... EVEN **VICIOUS!**

THERE'S NOTHING FUNNY ABOUT BELITTLING OTHERS FOR YOUR OWN ENJOYMENT! DO YOU HAVE TO MAKE OTHERS FEEL BAD SO THAT **YOU** CAN FEEL GOOD?

STARTING TODAY, I'M IMPOSING A NEW RULE: NO MORE COMICS ABOUT YOUR CLASSMATES!

OKAY? HAVE FUN.

Don't be mean!

Be perfect like me!

DUHH...

I DON'T MEAN TO BE "PICKY," BUT...

MR. ROS

Dang!

OW!

jug ears

BIG NATE by Lincoln Peirce

Teacher: NATE! WHAT ARE YOU DOING HERE?

Nate: SELLING COOKIES FOR MY SCOUT TROOP, MRS. GODFREY!

Teacher: SELLING COOKIES? WITH THE AMOUNT OF HOMEWORK I GAVE YOU THIS WEEKEND?

Nate: OH, RIGHT... THE HOMEWORK...

Teacher: I ASSUME YOU'VE FINISHED IT.

Nate: UH... WELL... NOT EXACTLY.

Teacher: NOT **EXACTLY**? HAVE YOU EVEN **STARTED** IT?

Nate: UH... **SURE** I HAVE! I'M... I'M ALMOST DONE!

Teacher: BUT YOU'RE **NOT** DONE! AND YET YOU'RE GALAVANTING AROUND THE NEIGHBORHOOD IN YOUR SCOUT UNIFORM!

Teacher: I GUESS YOU CARE MORE ABOUT SELLING **COOKIES** THAN YOU DO YOUR SOCIAL STUDIES GRADE!

Nate: WELL, I... **NO!** NO, NOT AT ALL!

Teacher: OH, REALLY? SO YOU'RE SAYING YOU'LL CHANGE YOUR WAYS? YOU'LL PUT YOUR HOMEWORK **FIRST** FROM NOW ON?

Nate: NOW YOU KNOW WHY SCOUTING TEACHES US SURVIVAL SKILLS!

Other scout: OH, HOW I HATE HER.

BIG NATE

by Lincoln Peirce

NATE!... **NATE! WAKE UP!**

HMM?

YOU WERE TALKING IN YOUR SLEEP!

SMAK! SMAK!

WHO DO YOU THINK YOU ARE, YOUNG MAN?

ME?

I GUESS I'M JUST ANOTHER STUDENT WHO'S BORED SILLY BY THIS LAME CLASS.

⌗ GASP! ⁑

NOBODY ELSE HAS THE GUTS TO SAY THIS, SO **I WILL**: MRS. GODFREY, YOUR LECTURES ARE ABOUT AS INTERESTING AS A BAG OF WET SAND.

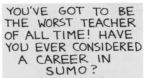

YOU'VE GOT TO BE THE WORST TEACHER OF ALL TIME! HAVE YOU EVER CONSIDERED A CAREER IN SUMO?

...AND FOR YOUR INFORMATION, I DO **NOT** TALK IN MY SLEEP!

ARE YOU SURE ABOUT THAT?

HMM? ABSOLUTELY.

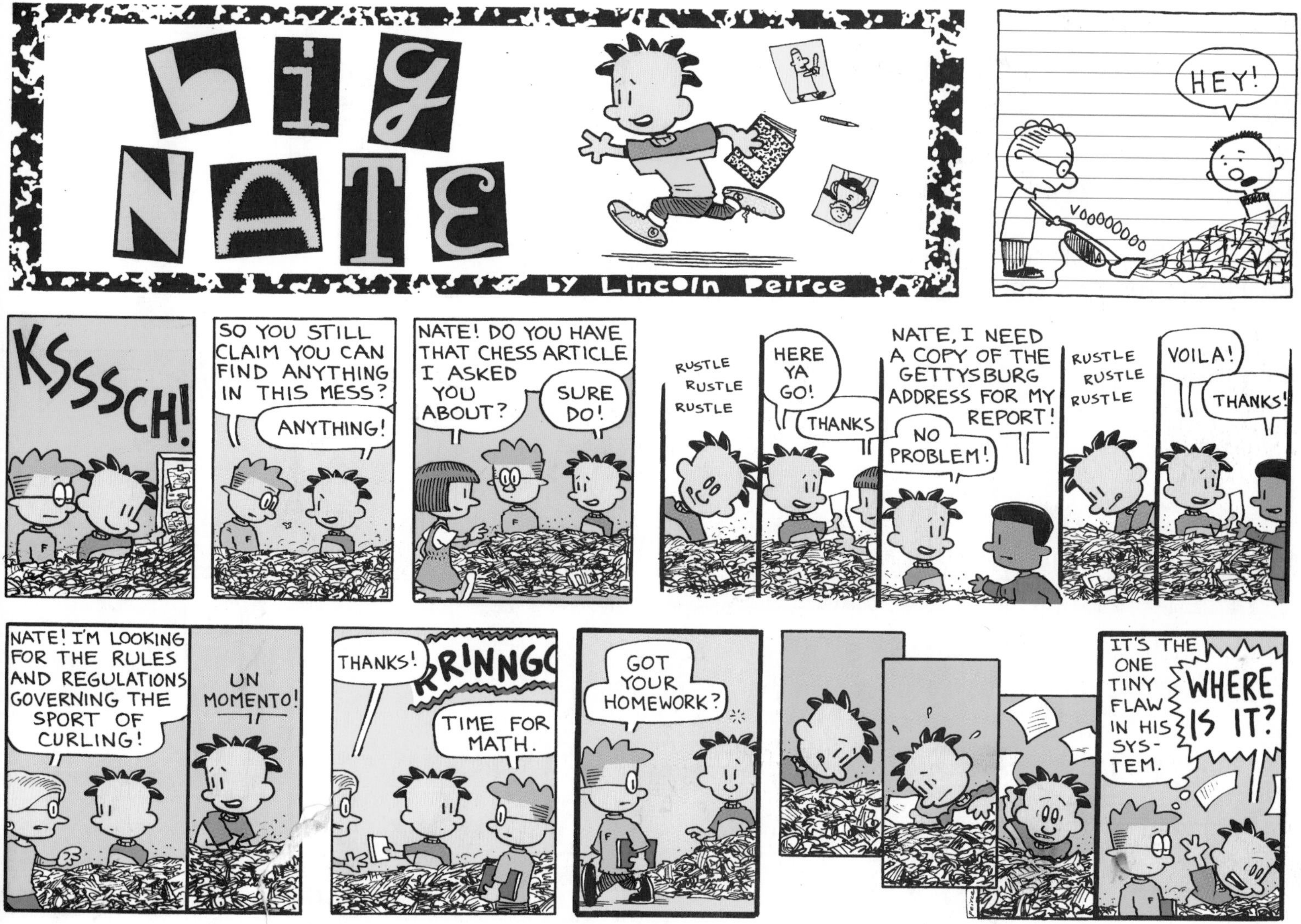
big NATE
by Lincoln Peirce
HEY!
VOOOOOOOO
KSSSCH!
SO YOU STILL CLAIM YOU CAN FIND ANYTHING IN THIS MESS?
ANYTHING!
NATE! DO YOU HAVE THAT CHESS ARTICLE I ASKED YOU ABOUT?
SURE DO!
RUSTLE RUSTLE RUSTLE
HERE YA GO!
THANKS
NATE, I NEED A COPY OF THE GETTYSBURG ADDRESS FOR MY REPORT!
NO PROBLEM!
RUSTLE RUSTLE RUSTLE
VOILA!
THANKS!
NATE! I'M LOOKING FOR THE RULES AND REGULATIONS GOVERNING THE SPORT OF CURLING!
UN MOMENTO!
THANKS!
RRINNGG
TIME FOR MATH.
GOT YOUR HOMEWORK?
IT'S THE ONE TINY FLAW IN HIS SYSTEM.
WHERE IS IT?

big NATE

by Lincoln Peirce

1.) Carl is taking a math test. There are 10 questions which take 30 seconds each; 15 questions which take 40 seconds each; and 12 questions which take two minutes each.

Carl pauses for 5 seconds between questions. In addition, he sharpens his pencil twice, which takes 20 seconds each time. The test begins promptly at 10:00 am. When Carl hands in his completed test,

what time is it?

YAAAAAAAH!

PRINCIPAL

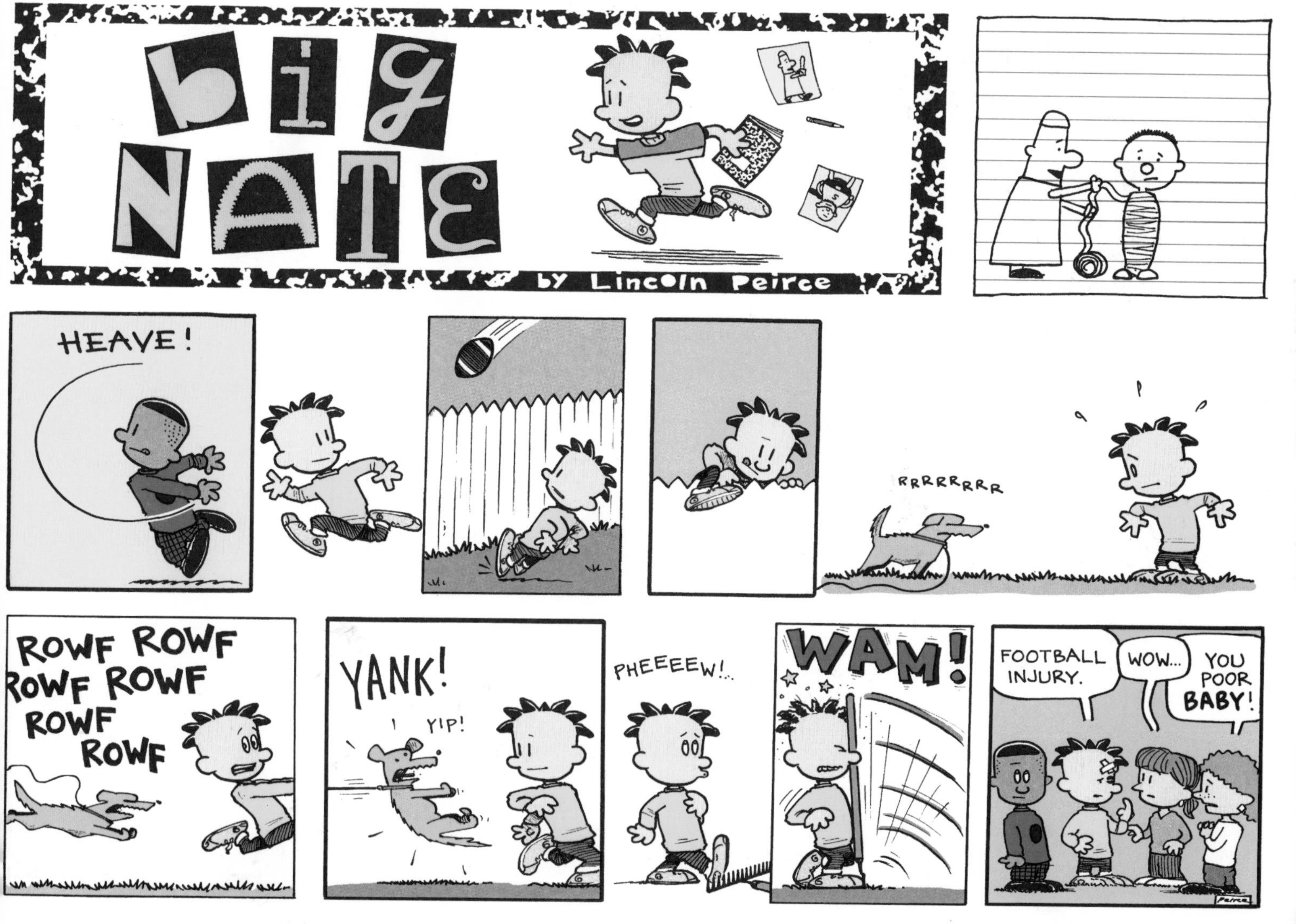
big NATE
by Lincoln Peirce
HEAVE!
RRRRRRRRR
ROWF ROWF ROWF ROWF ROWF ROWF
YANK!
YIP!
PHEEEEW!..
WAM!
FOOTBALL INJURY.
WOW...
YOU POOR BABY!
Peirce

BIG NATE

by Lincoln Peirce

Z...

* UP *
CLOSE
AND
PERSONAL!

with your
host:
CHIP
CHIPSON!

Greetings, friends!
I'm here with
"Cucurbita Pepo,"
or as he's more
commonly known...
**PAT
PUMPKIN!**

You da man, Chip.

Well, Pat, it's almost Halloween!

FINALLY! I'm sick of sitting around like a... a VEGETABLE!

So you look forward to this time of year, eh?

Oh, my Gourd, YES! It's the highlight of our year!

There's no greater honor for a pumpkin than getting picked, taken home and carved into a first-class Jack-o'-Lantern!

So it's not SCARY getting carved up?

Not at all! Unless... Unless...

Unless WHAT?

Unless you end up with a **CLUMSY CARVER!** You see, most people can easily carve a reasonably attractive pumpkin face...

...But there **ARE** a few hacks out there who don't know what they're doing! Getting carved by one of **THEM** is every pumpkin's greatest fear!

I HAD A LITTLE TROUBLE WITH THE MOUTH...

YOU'RE BLEEDING.

BIG NATE
by Lincoln Peirce

MMMM!... NATE'S HALLOWEEN CANDY!

JUST A LITTLE TREAT TO KEEP ME GOING...

WAIT A MINUTE! WHAT AM I THINKING?

bonk bonk

THE LAST THING THIS GUT NEEDS IS ANOTHER PIECE OF JUNK FOOD!

PAT PAT

STILL... IT WOULD JUST BE **ONE** PIECE...

WHO'S IT GOING TO HURT?

TRIP!

CLANG CLANG CLANG CLANG CLANG CLANG

OW.

PAY UP.

BIG NATE by Lincoln Peirce

Time For Another Edition Of....
CELEBRITY INTERVIEW!

with your host: *BIFF BIFFWELL!*

Greetings, friends! I'm here today with everyone's favorite gourd... JACK O'LANTERN, the Halloween pumpkin!!

groannn...

Jack, Halloween has been over for **TWO WEEKS**, and I'm sure a lot of folks are wondering: HOW are you doing?

How am I doing? How am I **DOING**?

I'm **ROTTING**, that's how I'm doing! My once-hard exterior is turning soft and slimy! I'm covered with **MOLD**!

Hmm... Yes, so I see...

Oh, **DO** you? You have no **IDEA** what we pumpkins go through!

We wait **ALL YEAR** for Halloween!.... And then, when it's over, what happens to us? We're **ABANDONED**!.... FORGOTTEN!

I can't **TAKE** it anymore! I'm gonna go out tonight and... and...

Get smashed?

I'm a shell of my former self.

BIG NATE by Lincoln Peirce

....AND ON THIS DATE IN HISTORY... UM... HMM.... LET'S SEE HERE...

☆ *Celebrity* ☆ **INTERVIEW!**

WITH YOUR HOST: *BIFF BIFFWELL!*

Hi again, friends! **BIFF BIFFWELL** here with our special guest: **NOVEMBER 15**TH!!

Salutations, Biff.

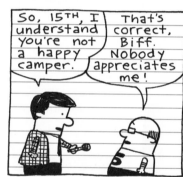

So, 15TH, I understand you're not a happy camper.

That's correct, Biff. Nobody appreciates me!

People always take notice of **OTHER** days in November: **ELECTION DAY!**... **VETERANS DAY!**... And of course that arrogant glory hound, **THANKSGIVING!**

But do people pay any attention to **ME? NO!** They say, "Oh, November 15th is just another day!"

But... **AREN'T** you just another day?

The point is, I could be so much **MORE!** I just need something to **HAPPEN!**

Like what?

ANYTHING! Anything **IMPORTANT!** Then people would start to recognize November 15th as a **SPECIAL DAY!**

"NOVEMBER 15TH: SCRUB TOILETS."

GREAT.

BIG NATE

by Lincoln Peirce

MAN! THAT NUMBER THIRTEEN IS **KILLING** US!

NATE, GET IN THERE AND GUARD NUMBER THIRTEEN.

HE'S EATING US UP, SO PLAY TOUGH, OK? TOUGH DEFENSE!

HOW?

I DON'T CARE HOW! JUST DENY HIM THE BALL! KEEP HIM FROM SCORING!

GOTCHA!

CLAP CLAP CLAP CLAP CLAP CLAP CLAP

YANK

I MAY HAVE TO START GETTING MORE SPECIFIC WITH MY COACHING INSTRUCTIONS.

NUMBER EIGHT, FLAGRANT WEDGIE.

SCORER

BIG NATE

by Lincoln Peirce

Greetings, fulfillment-seekers! Dr. **WARREN FUZZY** here, inviting **you** and **your mate** to take this quiz and ask yourselves:

ARE WE "CO-DEPENDENT"?

① When in public together, my mate and I:

SMAK SLURP — Oh, man! Not again! — horrified bystander

(A.) are proud to be seen in each other's company;
(B.) enjoy our mutual interests and hobbies with peers;
(C.) inevitably succumb to the urge to play "pass the gum."

② My mate and I get along so well because:

(A.) We respect and admire each other;
(B.) we share the same morals and values;
(C.) we wear matching outfits.

③ Before I met my mate, I was:

SWOON

(A.) happy and well-adjusted;
(B.) unaware I could love another person so much;
(C) I have repressed that entire meaningless time of my life from my memory.

④ Our other friends:

Who are THEY? — Beats me. — invisible bubble

(A.) are happy that we are so perfect together;
(B.) enjoy spending time with the two of us;
(C.) What are "other friends"?

⑤ The world would be a better place if:

(A.) we could eradicate hunger;
(B.) all wars would cease;
(C.) The world cannot get any better because the two of us will be together forever and ever!

...AND EVER... AND EVER...

OH, GORDIE...

HEY, **VELCRO COUPLE!** WANNA TAKE A QUIZ?

43

BIG NATE by Lincoln Peirce

...SO THEN THE DUCK SAYS TO THE ASTRONAUT...

HEY, WHAT ARE YOU DOING? CUT IT OUT!

I'M JUST GETTING THIS HAIR OFF YOUR SHOULDER...

WOW! A **LONG** HAIR! A **GIRL'S** HAIR!

OOOOH! GIVE ME THAT!

WHOSE HAIR IS IT, STUD?

WOULDN'T **YOU** LIKE TO KNOW!

COME ON, NATE! TELL US!

OH, I THINK I'LL JUST LET YOU **GUESS**! AFTER ALL, THERE ARE PLENTY OF POSSIBILITIES! **LOTS** OF CUTE GIRLS LIKE GETTING CLOSE TO ME!

✲ SNIFF! ✲ ...THIS FRAGRANT STRAND COULD HAVE COME FROM TINA, OR JULIE, OR SARAH...

I DON'T THINK SO...

THIS HAIR HAS SOME **GRAY** IN IT!

SOON I MAY BE GETTING A FEW GRAY ONES MYSELF.

BIG NATE by Lincoln Peirce

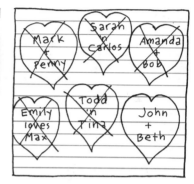

JOHN!... BETH!

HI, NATE!
YOU TWO ARE THE LONGEST-RUNNING COUPLE IN SCHOOL! CAN I INTERVIEW YOU FOR MY GOSSIP COLUMN, "CLASSROOM CHATTER"?

SURE!
GREAT! FIRST QUESTION: WHAT MAKES YOU SUCH A GREAT COUPLE?

WE JUST GET ALONG GREAT, THAT'S ALL! I'VE NEVER LIKED ANYONE AS MUCH AS I LIKE BETH!
NOT EVEN JULIE?

UH... JULIE?
EVERYONE KNOWS HOW HOT AND HEAVY YOU AND JULIE WERE BEFORE BETH MOVED TO TOWN!

NOT EVERY-ONE.
OH, YEAH! THE TWO OF THEM WERE LIKE VELCRO!

B-BUT THAT WAS A YEAR AGO!
YOU NEVER TOLD ME ANYTHING ABOUT JULIE! I DON'T KEEP SE-CRETS FROM YOU!
OH, YEAH? WHAT ABOUT KEVIN?
I'VE TOLD YOU A MILLION TIMES! WE WERE JUST FRIENDS!

I'LL JUST PUT "NO COMMENT."
HE'S THE TYPHOID MARY OF JOURNALISM.

45

BIG NATE

by Lincoln Peirce

THIS IS DRIVING ME CRAZY! I'VE HAD THIS SONG GOING THROUGH MY HEAD ALL DAY AND I CAN'T GET RID OF IT!

WHAT SONG?

NO! DON'T SAY IT!

THEN **WE'LL** BE INFECTED, TOO! I DON'T WANT SOME SONG STUCK IN MY HEAD!

HEY, I CAN SAY IT IF I WANT TO! IT'S...

NO!... OH SAY CAN YOU SEEE...

...BY THE DAWN'S EARLY LIIIIGHT...

WHAT SO PROUDLY WE HAILED...

OKAY. WHATEVER.

HA! SHOWED HIM!

WHOSE BROAD STRIPES AND BRIGHT STARS...

THRU THE PERILOUS FIGHT...

I'M AS PATRIOTIC AS THE NEXT GUY, BUT THIS IS RIDICULOUS.

...AND THE ROCKETS RED GLARE...

BIG NATE by Lincoln Peirce

boink!

NYUK NYUK NYUK!

WHAT DO YOU THINK, GORDIE?

HMMM...

YOUR ARTWORK IS DEFINITELY IMPROVING, NATE... BUT YOUR WRITING STILL NEEDS WORK!

EVER HEARD THE SAYING THAT BASEBALL IS 90% PITCHING? DRAWING A COMIC STRIP IS 90% **WRITING!**

A GOOD GAG IS THE FOUNDATION! THEN YOU CAN BUILD ON THAT FOUNDATION WITH YOUR ARTWORK!

THAT MAKES SENSE.

BUT IT'S EASY TO FORGET! SOMETIMES I START DRAWING A STRIP WITHOUT KNOWING HOW IT'LL END!

I GET TO THE LAST PANEL AND I REALIZE: HEY, I DON'T HAVE A PUNCHLINE HERE!

WOW. SO WHAT DO YOU DO THEN?

WELL, SOMETIMES I RESORT TO SLAPSTICK.

BUT... ISN'T THAT SORT OF CHEAP?

SORT OF, YEAH.

47

BIG NATE

by Lincoln Peirce

HAVE YOU EVER REALLY THOUGHT ABOUT HOW **UNFAIR** SCHOOL IS?

THE STUDENTS HAVE **NO RIGHTS!** IT'S THE **TEACHERS** WHO TELL US WHAT TO DO, WHEN TO DO IT, WHERE TO GO!

A BELL RINGS: WE GO TO HOMEROOM! ANOTHER BELL RINGS: WE GO TO LUNCH! ANOTHER BELL RINGS! WE GO TO SOCIAL STUDIES!

ALL THESE BELLS ARE THEIR WAY TO **CONTROL** US! **THEY'RE** THE GUARDS! **WE'RE** THE PRISONERS!

I NEVER THOUGHT OF IT THAT WAY...

RRRRIIIINNNGG

OOP! TIME FOR MATH!

NO! DON'T GO!

RRRRRRRRRRRRIIIIIIIIIIINNNNNNNGGGGGGGG

IGNORE THAT BELL! TAKE BACK CONTROL OF YOUR LIVES!!

OH, NATE! YOU'RE WONDERFUL!

RRRIIIIIIIIIIIINNNNNNNNGGGGGGGGG

STAND YOUR GROUND!

NATE!... NATE!... **NATE!**

NATE! NATE!

BIG NATE

by Lincoln Peirce

DANG!

HA! THAT'S AN "E"!

JUST ONE MORE LETTER AND YOU LOSE!

I KNOW, I KNOW.

YESSS! MAKE **THAT** ONE, PAL!

RATS!

THAT'S IT! THAT'S A "Y"!

G-O-D-F-R-E-Y!

♪ FRANCIS IS A GODFREY!... FRANCIS IS A GODFREY! ♪

OH, THE **HORROR!** COULD THERE BE **ANYTHING** WORSE THAN BEING A GODFRE—

!

MY DAD SAYS THAT WHEN HE WAS A KID, THEY CALLED IT "HORSE."

DETENTION

49

BIG NATE by Lincoln Peirce

HOW MUCH WILL YOU GIVE ME IF I HIT THAT TREE?

THAT TREE? IT'S LIKE A HUNDRED YARDS AWAY!

WILL YOU GIVE ME TEN BUCKS?

NO, I WON'T GIVE YOU TEN BUCKS!

FIVE BUCKS?

I DON'T HAVE ANY MONEY! BESIDES, YOU COULD NEVER REACH THAT TREE!

HOW ABOUT THIS:

IF I HIT THAT TREE WITH **THIS** SNOWBALL, I GET TO HIT **YOU** WITH **ANOTHER** SNOWBALL!

FINE. YOU WON'T HIT THAT TREE IN A MILLION YEARS.

HERE GOES.

POW!

BY GOLLY, YOU'RE RIGHT! I WASN'T EVEN **CLOSE**!

BIG NATE

by Lincoln Peirce

Panel 1:
NATE: I WANT TO FIGURE OUT HOW TO DRAW CARICATURES.

TEACHER: I TOOK A CLASS ABOUT THAT ONCE! I'LL GIVE YOU SOME TIPS!

Panel 2:
ALL PEOPLE HAVE CERTAIN FEATURES THAT MAKE THEM STAND OUT! I'VE GOT A SQUARE HEAD AND A CROOKED NOSE! YOU'VE GOT SPIKY HAIR!

Panel 3:
AS A CARICATURIST, YOU TRY TO **EXAGGERATE** THOSE FEATURES!

NATE: SO IF SOMEONE HAS A BIG NOSE, YOU DRAW IT **HUGE**! GOTCHA!

Panel 4:
NATE: OOH! GORDIE! DRAW A CARICATURE OF ELLEN!

TEACHER: OKAY! WELL, OBVIOUSLY I'LL START WITH—

Panel 5:

Panel 6:
ACTUALLY, ELLEN'S FEATURES ARE SO FLAWLESS THAT A CARICATURE OF HER JUST WOULDN'T WORK.

Panel 7:
SEE YOU, NATE.

Panel 8:
NO SPINE

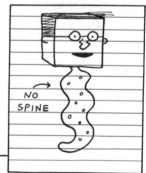

BIG NATE

by Lincoln Peirce

!

WHOA! **WHOA**, MR. EUSTIS! WHAT ARE YOU DOING?

I'M ABOUT TO SHOVEL MY DRIVEWAY.

SAVE YOURSELF THE LABOR, MR. EUSTIS! HIRE "N.F.T. YARDCARE"!

I'LL SHOVEL YOU OUT FOR TEN BUCKS!

THANKS, BUT NO, THANKS.

AW, HOW COME? WHY DO IT YOUR**SELF** WHEN **I'M** HERE?

AFTER ALL, YOU **HAVE** AVAILED YOURSELF OF MY SERVICES **BEFORE**!

YES, I KNOW.

FWOOSH!

AS I RECALL, I HIRED YOU TO RAKE MY LEAVES **THREE WEEKS AGO**!

YOU KNOW, YOU WERE NEXT ON MY LIST...

BiG NATE

by Lincoln Peirce

Howdy, friends! *BIFF BIFFWELL* here with another edition of...

WHAT'S YOUR JOB?

Here's our first guest, HOWARD PLOTZ! Tell us, Howard: "What's your job?"

Resolution accountant, Biff.

Hmm... What does that involve?

Well, Biff, at this time of the season, millions of people are making New Year's resolutions!

And you keep track of them?

Right! As you can see, my ledger has two columns: resolutions **KEPT** and resolutions **BROKEN**!

Seems like a pretty big job for one guy!

Oh, it is. I can't possibly keep up with the numbers by myself!

That's why I employ a world-wide network of helpers to act as my eyes and ears!

You have **SPIES**?

Hey, **SOME**one's got to be there when a resolution gets broken!

AH HA!

OOPS

WELL? HOW'D IT GO?

GREAT!

I NAILED HIM POINT-BLANK WITH THREE SNOWBALLS!

HEE HEE!

THAT'LL TEACH NATE NOT TO CHALLENGE ME TO ANY MORE SNOWBALL FIGHTS!

HE HAS ABSOLUTELY **NO CLUE** ABOUT THE ART OF WAR!

HE HAS NO CUNNING! NO BATTLE INSTINCTS WHATSOEVER!

LIKE THE WAY I USED **YOU** AS A DOUBLE AGENT! SHEER GENIUS! YOU THINK **HE'D** EVER THINK UP A PLAN LIKE THAT?

I'M NOT SURE...

WHY DON'T YOU ASK HIM?

YAAAA

CLIK!

COCOA?

LOVE SOME!

big NATE

by Lincoln Peirce

PASS! PASS!

WHUMP!

PTOO!

STOMP!!

!

zinnngg

oof!

grunt!

zinnggggg.

FWING!

SLUP!

SWISH!

JUST THE WAY I DIAGRAMED IT.

I GET AN ASSIST FOR THAT, RIGHT?

big NATE

by Lincoln Peirce

ALMANACS
1¢

♪

MAN, THAT SOCIAL STUDIES TEST WAS A **BREEZE!**

SOME OF THOSE QUESTIONS WERE SO **EASY!** WE'RE TALKING TOTAL SLAM DUNKS!

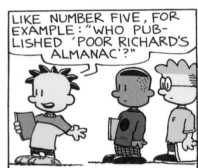

LIKE NUMBER FIVE, FOR EXAMPLE: "WHO PUBLISHED 'POOR RICHARD'S ALMANAC'?"

I MEAN... **DUH!** THAT'S LIKE "WHO'S BURIED IN GRANT'S TOMB?"

OBVIOUSLY THE PUBLISHER OF "POOR RICHARD'S ALMANAC" WAS **POOR RICHARD!**

WHAT DID HE MEAN, "POOR NATE"?

FIGURE IT OUT.

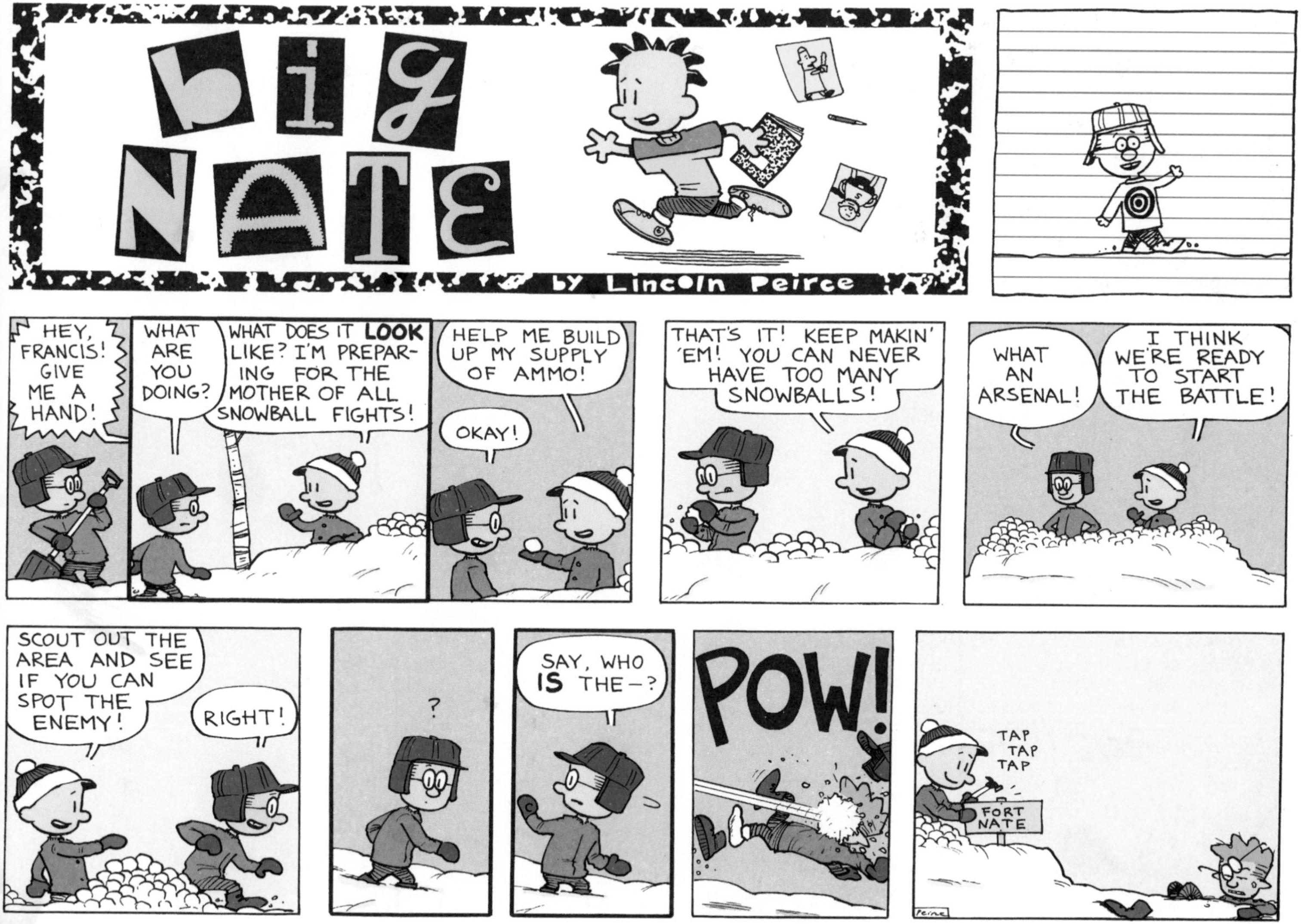
big NATE
by Lincoln Peirce
HEY, FRANCIS! GIVE ME A HAND!
WHAT ARE YOU DOING?
WHAT DOES IT **LOOK** LIKE? I'M PREPARING FOR THE MOTHER OF ALL SNOWBALL FIGHTS!
HELP ME BUILD UP MY SUPPLY OF AMMO!
OKAY!
THAT'S IT! KEEP MAKIN' 'EM! YOU CAN NEVER HAVE TOO MANY SNOWBALLS!
WHAT AN ARSENAL!
I THINK WE'RE READY TO START THE BATTLE!
SCOUT OUT THE AREA AND SEE IF YOU CAN SPOT THE ENEMY!
RIGHT!
?
SAY, WHO **IS** THE—?
POW!
TAP TAP TAP
FORT NATE

by Lincoln Peirce

WHOA! WHOA! HALT!

WHAT'S **YOUR** PROBLEM?

YOU ARE MY PROBLEM! YOU AND YOUR **FIGURE SKATES!**

WE'RE PLAYING HOCKEY HERE, ELLEN! **HOCKEY!**

WE CAN'T HAVE YOU HACKING UP OUR RINK WITH YOUR LITTLE PICKS!

FIGURE SKATING IS AN **ABOMINATION!** IT'S AN INSULT TO ICE EVERYWHERE!

CAN ANYONE TELL ME WHY FIGURE SKATES WERE EVEN INVENTED IN THE **FIRST PLACE?**

POINK!

YOWOWOWOW!!

OOH! TRIPLE AXEL!

LOUSY FORM THOUGH.

by Lincoln Peirce

ZAP!

OKAY... MAGIC MOMENT COMING UP HERE...

JENNY'S MY PARTNER ON THIS SCIENCE PROJECT... OUR ARMS ARE ONLY INCHES APART...

ALL I NEED TO DO IS CASUALLY MOVE A BIT TO THE LEFT...

OUR HANDS WILL TOUCH... OUR EYES WILL MEET... DESTINY!!

OW!

POP!

WHOOPS... SORRY...

WHAT ARE YOU **DOING**, YOU IDIOT? YOU GAVE ME AN ELECTRIC **SHOCK!**

HEH HEH... I...UH... THAT IS...

?! YOU'RE **LAUGHING**?? YOU THINK THIS IS FUNNY? IS THIS **FUNNY** TO YOU?

POW!

WHAT'S WITH NATE'S HAIR?

MUST BE STATIC.

59

BIG NATE by Lincoln Peirce

HOLD IT, TEDDY!

WHOA! **WHOA!** WHAT ARE YOU **DOING?**

HAVING A SNOWBALL FIGHT WITH FRANCIS... **AS IF** YOU DIDN'T KNOW!

WHAT'S THAT SUPPOSED TO MEAN?

DON'T PLAY INNOCENT! I FELL FOR THAT **LAST** TIME!

OH. YOU MEAN WHEN I AMBUSHED YOU WHILE WORKING AS FRANCIS' DOUBLE AGENT?

DUH! YOU'RE OBVIOUSLY WORKING FOR HIM **AGAIN!**

YOU'RE JUST **ASSUMING** THAT! WHAT IF YOU'RE **WRONG?**

HUH?

HOW DO YOU KNOW I'M WORKING FOR **FRANCIS?** HOW DO YOU KNOW I'M NOT WORKING FOR **YOU?**

HMM... THAT'S RIGHT. MAYBE YOU **ARE** WORKING FOR ME...

HEY, BUT **WAIT** A MINUTE! IF YOU **WERE** WORKING FOR ME, WOULDN'T I—?

POW!

JUST FOR THE RECORD, I'M NOT WORKING FOR YOU.

CAN WE PLAY SOMETHING ELSE? THIS IS TOO EASY.

BY Lincoln Peirce

DAD? WILL YOU TELL ME THAT MOVIE STORY AGAIN?

WHAT MOVIE STORY?

YOU KNOW... ABOUT WHEN YOU WERE A KID... GOING TO THE MATINEE...

AH! YOU MEAN THE "CREATURE FEATURE"!

EVERY SATURDAY, MY BEST FRIEND JERRY PITTS AND I WOULD RIDE OUR BIKES DOWN TO THE OLD STRAND THEATRE!...

FOR TWO BUCKS YOU COULD WATCH A HORROR MOVIE, EAT A POPCORN AND DRINK A SODA! ALL WHILE SITTING IN THE BALCONY! THOSE WERE THE DAYS!

ALL THAT FOR TWO DOLLARS? YOWZA!

HARD TO BELIEVE, ISN'T IT?

BUT WHERE'D YOU GET THE MONEY?

FROM MY FATH—

..ER

$

THE MOVIE'S ON DAD, GRAMPS!

ABOUT TIME.

BIG NATE
by Lincoln Peirce

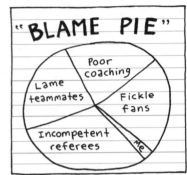

COME ON, 'CATS! PICK UP THE PACE!

YOU CUT TO THE LEFT! YOU WERE **SUPPOSED** TO CUT TO THE **RIGHT**!

HE FOULED ME! HE WAS ALL OVER ME!

COVER THAT GUY! **COVER** HIM!

WAKE UP, MARSHALL! PLAY YOUR POSITION!

BUZZZZZZ

ME?

WHY ARE YOU TAKING **ME** OUT? TAKE OUT ONE OF **THEM**!

HE'S REDEFINING THE ROLE OF "POINT" GUARD.

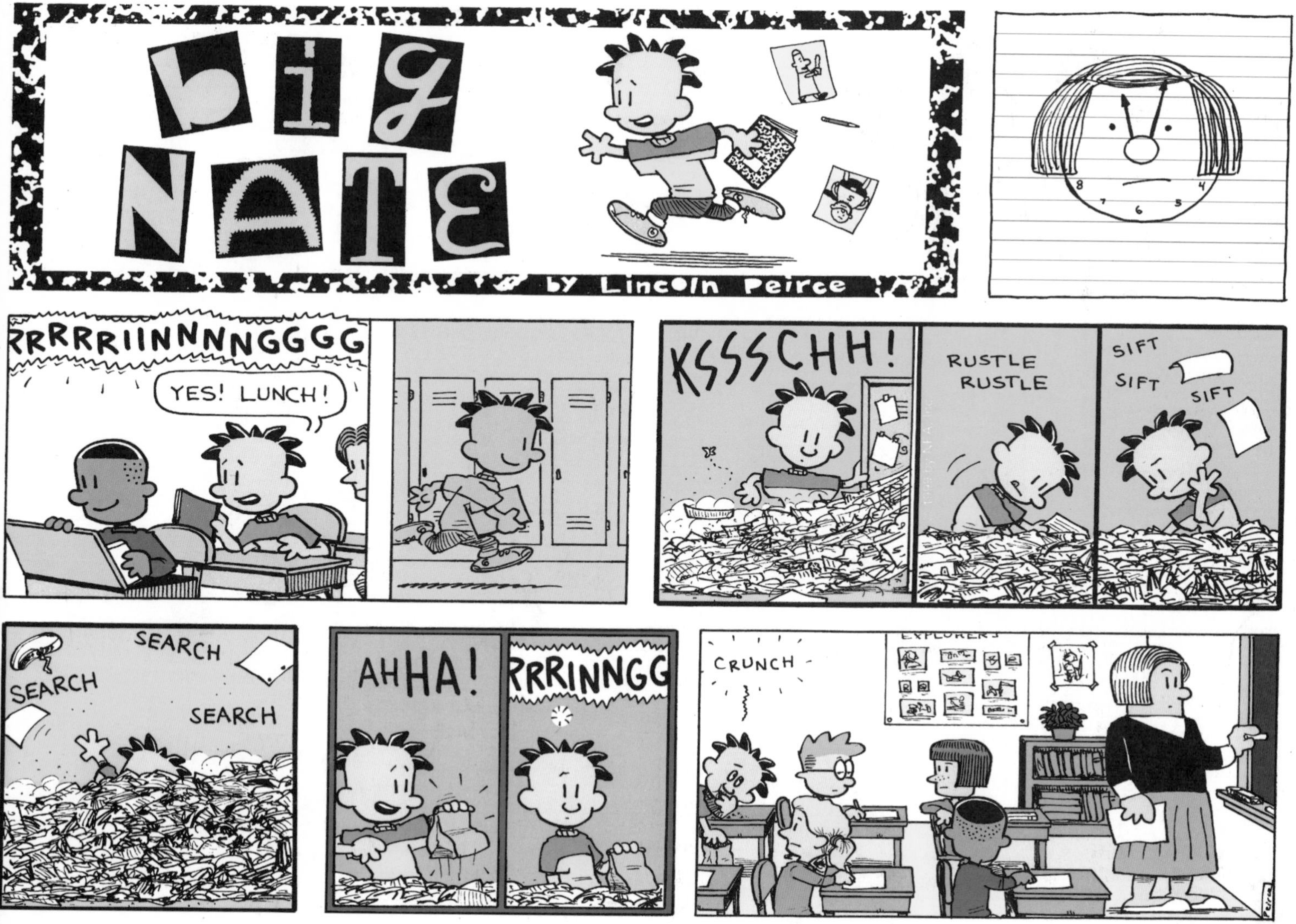
big NATE
by Lincoln Peirce
RRRRRIINNNNNGGGG
YES! LUNCH!
KSSSCHH!
RUSTLE RUSTLE
SIFT
SIFT
SIFT
SEARCH
SEARCH
SEARCH
AHHA!
RRRINNGG
CRUNCH

big NATE
by Lincoln Peirce
Test Your Knowledge!
Test Your Skill!
TAKE THE...
Mrs. GODFREY "FUN FACTS" QUIZ!
1. Mrs. Godfrey became a social studies instructor because:
You'll never amount to anything.
A. A career as a ballet dancer just didn't pan out.
B. She loves useless facts about obscure 16th century explorers.
C. She enjoys ~~warping~~ teaching young people.
2. Mrs. Godfrey's middle initial, B, stands for:
DAD
A. Beth
B. Barbara
C. Beelzebub
3. Mrs. Godfrey's favorite perfume is called:
oolp!
what a stench!
A. "Charlie"
B. "Myron"
C. "Dead Fish"
4. Which of the following can be found in Mrs. Godfrey's desk:
what are YOU looking at?
A. Breath mints
B. "Sweatin' To The Oldies" tape
C. Magazine article entitled "Rodents: Our Misunderstood Cousins"
5. "1776" refers to:
A. The signing of The Declaration of Independence.
B. Washington crossing the Delaware.
C. Mrs. Godfrey's weight.
6. When not behind her desk, Mrs. Godfrey can be found:
DO NOT DISTURB
A. At the candy machine in the teachers' lounge.
B. Performing her twice-daily eyebrow trimming.
C. Under a nearby rock.
PERSONALLY, I'D PUT "C" FOR NUMBER SIX!
UH.... I'LL JUST PUT "NONE OF THE ABOVE."
PEIRCE

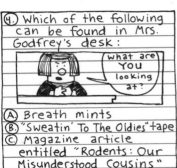

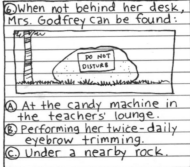

BIG NATE

BY Lincoln Peirce

OH, **NO!** WHAT'S **HE** DOING HERE?

THAT GUY? HE'S HERE TO TAKE PHOTOS!

YOU KNOW, ACTION SHOTS! DURING THE GAME!

AAARRGH! COULDN'T SOMEBODY **ELSE** DO IT? THAT GUY IS MY **NEMESIS!**

HE TAKES OUR CLASS PHOTOS EVERY YEAR AND ALWAYS CATCHES ME WITH THE **STUPIDEST** LOOK ON MY FACE!

THAT'S BECAUSE YOU'RE **POSING!** YOU'RE SELF-CONSCIOUS!

BUT YOU WON'T HAVE THAT PROBLEM DURING THE **GAME!** YOU'LL BE TOO BUSY **PLAYING!**

TWEET!

HMM.. YOU'RE RIGHT!

BZZZZZZZ

TIME OUT, HOME TEAM!

WHEW! WATER!

HEY! MY RETAINER'S IN THERE!

PTOO!

KLIK!

Big NATE
by Lincoln Peirce

PLEASE RECYCLE CLAY!

HUM HUMMM HUM DE DUM...

GOOD MORNING, MRS. GODFREY!

WHAT'S GOOD ABOUT IT, NATE?

I COMPLETED THE HOMEWORK, MA'AM!

GIVE ME THAT!

HMM... NATE, THIS IS EXTRAORDINARY WORK. BUT SINCE I DON'T LIKE YOU, I'M GIVING YOU A "D."

BUT THAT'S NOT FAIR!

ASK ME IF I CARE, KID! NYA HA HA HA HA HA!

MRS. GODFREY! LOOK OUT!

HMM?

WHAM!

OOPS.

NATE, ISN'T IT TIME FOR YOUR VISIT WITH THE SCHOOL COUNSELOR?

BIG NATE

by Lincoln Peirce

BRAVO!

6.0

AARRGH! FIGURE SKATING **AGAIN**?

YUP!

HOW CAN YOU WATCH THIS SCHLOCK?

IT'S NOT SCHLOCK! IT'S **EXCITING**!

AND IT'S **BEAUTIFUL**, TOO! LOOK AT TATIANA! SHE'S SO **GRACEFUL**!

GRACEFUL? SHE LOOKS LIKE SHE'S BEING AT-TACKED BY HORNETS!

THAT'S CALLED **CHOREO-GRAPHY**, IDIOT!

NICE **COSTUME**, TOO! WHAT DID SHE DO, ROLL AROUND ON THE FLOOR OF A SEQUIN FACTORY?

RRINNG!

HELLO?... OH, HI, FRANCIS... YUP, YOU CERTAINLY MAY SPEAK TO NATE.

LET ME GO GET HIM. HE'S WATCHING FIGURE SKATING.

NO!

OOP. HERE HE IS NOW.

big NATE by Lincoln Peirce

Above... dove... glove... muv... nuv... puv... luv...

✂AHEM✂

MY LOVE IS LIKE A RED, RED ROSE THAT BLOOMS WITH PETALS SWEET. MY LOVE, LIKE MOUNT ST. HELENS, GLOWS WITH AWE-INSPIRING HEAT.

MY LOVE IS LIKE A PERFECT PEARL PLUCKED FROM AN OYSTER PRIME. MY LOVE IS LIKE A FUZZY SQUIRREL (I HAD TO MAKE IT RHYME).

MY LOVE JUST CANNOT BE DENIED, CANNOT BE STOPPED OR SQUELCHED. IT'S LIKE A SIGH THAT MUST BE SIGHED, A BURP THAT MUST BE BELCHED.

YOU'VE DATED MANY OTHER GUYS. (EXCUSE ME WHILE I YAWN.) THEY'RE LIKE A BURGER, SHAKE AND FRIES, WHILE I'M FILET MIGNON.

UNTIL YOU STOP IGNORING ME, UNTIL WE HAVE A DATE, UNTIL TO LOVE ME YOU AGREE, I'M YOURS SINCERELY... NATE.

HEAR THAT, JENNY? THAT WAS FOR **YOU**!

OKAY, NOW FOR THIS MORNING'S ANNOUNCEMENTS...

BIG NATE by Lincoln Peirce

PEACE ← | QUIET →

TEACHERS' LOUNGE! SEE THAT? **TEACHERS' LOUNGE!**

HOW COME **THEY** GET A ROOM TO HANG OUT IN AND **WE DON'T?**

WE'RE THE ONES WHO REALLY **NEED** A PLACE LIKE THAT! **WE'RE** THE ONES WHO ARE UNDER ALL THE **STRESS!**

WHILE THEY'RE IN THERE EATING DONUTS AND TAKING CATNAPS, WE'RE OUT HERE RUNNING AROUND LIKE RATS IN A MAZE!

IS IT ASKING TOO MUCH FOR US TO HAVE A PLACE FOR OURSELVES?...WHERE WE CAN **RELAX** FOR A CHANGE?

JUST GIVE US A **ROOM**, THAT'S ALL! I MEAN, DON'T WE **DESERVE** THAT? **DON'T WE??**

ALL I WANT IS A LITTLE PEACE AND—

QUIET PLEASE   DETENTION

BIG NATE

by Lincoln Peirce

OOOH, MAN, WHAT A **GAME**! I MEAN, WE LOST AND EVERYTHING, BUT **I** DID PRETTY WELL!

ESPECIALLY SINCE IT WAS MY FIRST GAME BACK! NO RUST ON **ME**, NO **SIR**!

DON'T YOU THINK I LOOKED PRETTY GOOD OUT THERE, FRANCIS?

HMM? WHAT'S THIS?

TWO WORDS... FIRST WORD: SOUNDS LIKE... BIG?... HIGH?... TALL?... **TALL**!

FALL? WALL? BALL? **BALL**!

SECOND WORD... UMMM... NOSE? BALL **NOSE**? NO... WHAT?... BIG NOSE? NO... **PIG** NOSE?

SECOND WORD **PIG**? NO... WHAT?... HOG? SECOND WORD HOG?... BALL... HOG?

BALL HOG!

SNAP SNAP

I'M A BALL HOG?

OKAY, WHATEVER. BUT DID I LOOK PRETTY GOOD OUT THERE OR WHAT?

HE'S YET TO GRASP THE CONCEPT OF THE "SILENT TREATMENT."

AND WHAT'S WITH THE CHARADES THING?

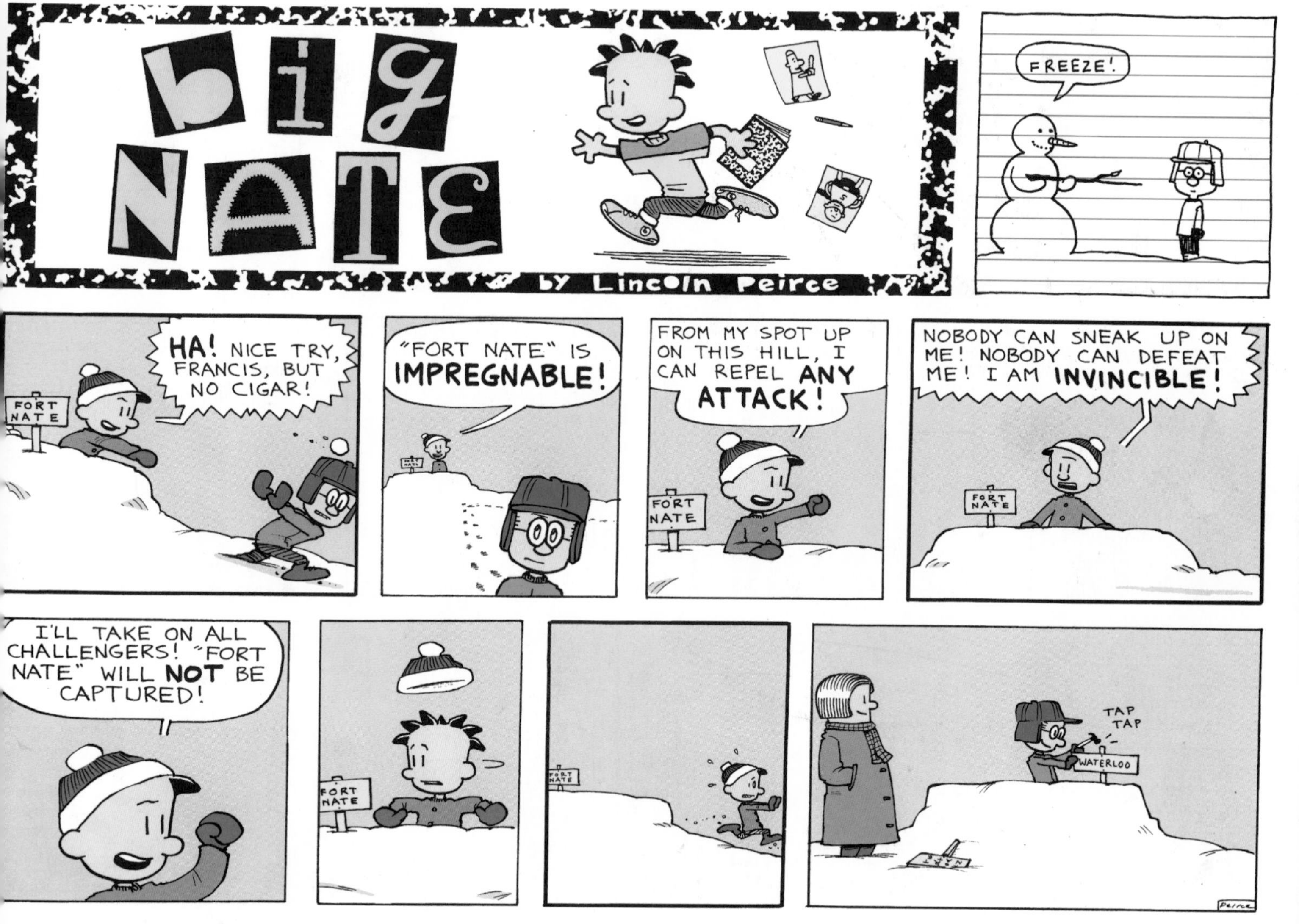
big NATE
by Lincoln Peirce
FREEZE!
HA! NICE TRY, FRANCIS, BUT NO CIGAR!
FORT NATE
"FORT NATE" IS IMPREGNABLE!
FROM MY SPOT UP ON THIS HILL, I CAN REPEL ANY ATTACK!
FORT NATE
NOBODY CAN SNEAK UP ON ME! NOBODY CAN DEFEAT ME! I AM INVINCIBLE!
FORT NATE
I'LL TAKE ON ALL CHALLENGERS! "FORT NATE" WILL NOT BE CAPTURED!
FORT NATE
TAP TAP
WATERLOO
PEIRCE

BIG NATE by Lincoln Peirce

WHAT'S NEW IN THE ART ROOM?

IT'S STILL LIFE WEEK!

WHY SO MANY?

BECAUSE I LET THE STUDENTS CREATE THEIR **OWN** STILL LIFES!

IT'S MUCH MORE INTERESTING THAN HAVING THEM PAINT STILL LIFES THAT **I** SET UP!

THIS WAY, THEY'RE PAINTING THINGS THAT ARE **SIGNIFICANT** TO THEM! THEY TAKE OWNERSHIP OF THEIR ARTWORK!

IT'S FUN FOR **ME**, TOO! I CAN LOOK AT THESE STILL LIFES AND TRY TO FIGURE OUT WHAT THESE KIDS ARE ALL ABOUT!

SOME OF THEM ARE EASIER TO DECODE THAN OTHERS.

COMIN' THROUGH! MY STILL LIFE NEEDS MORE CHEEZ DOODLES!

by Lincoln Peirce

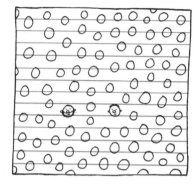

Time Once Again For The Adventures Of...

SUPERDAD!

...The world's **ONLY** bald super-hero with a slight paunch!

One day at **SUPERDAD'S** secret headquarters...

RRRRRINNNG!

EGAD! It's the HOTLINE!

What's that, Commissioner? You say it's **SNOWING** outside?

ZOUNDS! You're RIGHT!

This can only mean **ONE THING**: the **DRIVEWAY** needs to be SHOVELED!

DRAMATIC MUSIC

THIS is a job for...

Hmm... That looks like **wet** snow!... **Heavy** snow!

My back's been a little tender lately...

Plus, I've got this nasty hang-nail!

...But this shoveling **MUST** be done!

There's **GOT** to be a way!

BIG NATE

by Lincoln Peirce

Time Once Again, Friends, To Open...

Dan Cupid's MAIL BAG!

Hello again, gang! Today's first letter is from **NATE** and **ELLEN WRIGHT**, a brother and sister who ask: " Dan, please bring some **ROMANCE** into our father's life!"

At first, this seems like a SIMPLE REQUEST! **BUT**... watch what happens!

CLOUD 9

CLOUD 7

CLOUD 3

First, I shoot Nate and Ellen's Dad with one of my official **LOVE DARTS®**! He is now ready for love! He is **SUSCEPTIBLE**!

SPROING!

But when I search for a **MATE** for Dad, there's trouble! **WHY**? Because Dad has no **LIFE**! He never **GOES** anywhere!

It's hard to find someone to hook up with Dad when all he does is sit around the house!

The result: Dad, still under the spell of my **LOVE DART®**, now inappropriately transfers his affections **ELSEWHERE**!

ISN'T "THE NANNY" THE CUTEST THING?

SAD.

PATHETIC.

BIG NATE

by Lincoln Peirce

Letters! He gets **Letters**!

DAN CUPID'S VALENTINE **MAILBAG**!!

Well, friends, it's that time of year again, and the mail from lonely hearts has **REALLY** been piling up!

As the world's #1 matchmaker, I can say with confidence that I'll be able to find mates for **ALMOST** all these people!

Why "**ALMOST**," you ask? Simply put, there is a small group of folks out there with **NO CHANCE** of finding love!

← example

Yes, it's tragic... but there **IS** something I can do!

Looove... Exciting and new...

Watch carefully as I aim two love darts: the first at the lonely person; and the second at... well... whatever's handy!

sproing!

sproing!

It might not be true love between two human beings, but it's better than **NOTHING**!

BIG NATE
by Lincoln Peirce

WHAT'S THAT FOR? I'VE WRITTEN A VALENTINE SONG FOR JENNY!

I'M PULLING OUT ALL THE STOPS TO SHOW HER THAT SHE'S THE ONLY ONE FOR ME!

♪ OH JENNY... YOU'RE SO FIIINE! WILL YOU BE MY VALENTIIINE?...

PLINK! PLUNK!

OH WO JEN— ♫

OOP! HI.

!

JENNY AND HER FAMILY ARE OUT OF TOWN.

I'M HOUSE-SITTING.

OH. OKAY.

DANG! SHE'S NOT HOME!

TOO BAD.

YOUR SONG WILL GO TO WASTE.

OOH! HEY! YOU! WHAT'S YOUR NAME?

YEAH, YOU! WHAT'S YOUR NAME?

PATTY

♪ OH PATTY... YOU'RE SO FIIINE!...

HE'S VERY ADAPTABLE.

BIG NATE
by Lincoln Peirce

creak!

Hey, Gang! Let's play...

"PEERLESS®"!

Directions: Help personality-challenged teen **ELLEN WRIGHT** find the **PEER GROUP** that's just right for her!

vacant stare

START

Group #1: JOCKS!

Dang! Broke my collarbone!

Tore my ACL!

I've got really bad acne!

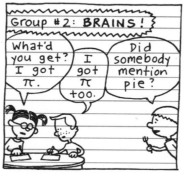

Group #2: BRAINS!

What'd you get? I got π.

I got π too.

Did somebody mention pie?

Group #3: DEBS!

Hi, girls!

Just ignore her. Just ignore her.

Group #4: PERFORMERS!

FAME!... I wanna live forever...

I can catch a frisbee in my teeth!

Hello?

Group #5: FREAKS!

Okay, wait a sec... What's the difference between "Deep Space Nine" and "Babylon 5"?

GASP!

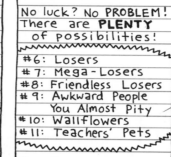

No luck? No PROBLEM! There are **PLENTY** of possibilities!

#6: Losers
#7: Mega-Losers
#8: Friendless Losers
#9: Awkward People You Almost Pity
#10: Wallflowers
#11: Teachers' Pets

※URK!※

HOW ABOUT "ENRAGED SISTERS"?

BIG NATE by Lincoln Peirce

16 TONS

Time Once Again FOR...

CELEBRITY INTERVIEW!

Here's your host: **CHIP CHIPSON!**

Greetings, friends! We're chatting with love-meister **DAN CUPID** about the yearly madness known as **SPRING FEVER!**

What's the word, Chip?

Let's start with the basics, Dan: **WHY** is **SPRING** known far and wide as the "season of love"?

CUPID TRAINING, Chip!

When Spring arrives, hundreds of apprentice cupids graduate from our "Love Academy" and begin their training period "in the field"!

This is the first time these trainees have had a chance to use actual "love darts" on real people!

As you might expect, they want to earn their stripes! So they shoot at anything that MOVES! Even if that target has **ALREADY BEEN HIT!**

But... doesn't that cause problems?

Well... yes, it **CAN** get ugly...

HIIIIII...

HI

HEY!

BIG NATE

by Lincoln Peirce

1823 - Monroe ~~Doctk~~ Doctrine
Pres. Monroe opposed to Euro NATE!
Dr. Cesspool

MAJOR STUDY SESSION!

OKAY, HERE'S ANOTHER ONE:

BRIEFLY DESCRIBE WHAT THE "MONROE DOCTRINE" WAS.

HMMM... WELL, WHATEVER IT WAS, IT OBVIOUSLY INVOLVED SOME GUY NAMED MONROE...

MONROE **DOCTRINE**, YOU SAID? SO THAT MEANS HE WAS A **DOCTOR**, MAYBE... RIGHT? BUT I DON'T REMEMBER ANY DOCTORS IN MY CLASS NOTES...

BUT **SPEAKING** OF DOCTORS... (HEE HEE!)... WANNA SEE MY LATEST "DOCTOR CESSPOOL" COMIC? HE AMPUTATES THIS GUY'S FOOT, SEE, AND THEN... **OH!**

THAT REMINDS ME! DID YOU SEE JEFF BRINKER'S FOOT AFTER PHYS.ED ON FRIDAY? THE THING WAS THE SIZE OF A **BASKETBALL**! ALL SWOLLEN AND BRUISED AND—

WHAT WAS THE QUESTION?

HE USUALLY DOES BETTER WITH "MULTIPLE CHOICE."

by Lincoln Peirce

SIXTY YEARS FROM NOW...

When did Ponce de Leon arrive in Florida?

Hey, ask me if I care!

OKAY, HERE'S MY POINT...

NOBODY EVER LOOKS BACK ON THEIR LIFE AND REGRETS THAT THEY DIDN'T DO MORE HOMEWORK!

DO OLD PEOPLE SIT AROUND SAYING, "GOSH, I WISH I'D DONE THAT SOCIAL STUDIES HOMEWORK SIXTY YEARS AGO"?

NO! THEY WISH THEY'D SPENT MORE TIME HAVING FUN! PLAYING! DOING STUFF THEY ACTUALLY LIKE TO DO!

I HAPPEN TO UNDERSTAND THAT! I'M NOT GOING TO FRITTER AWAY THE BEST YEARS OF MY LIFE HELD HOSTAGE BY SCHOOL!

HAND 'EM IN, PEOPLE.

TEMPUS FUGIT

DETENTION

80

BIG NATE by Lincoln Peirce

"SCHOOL DAYS"

P.S. 38 PARENTS NIGHT 6:00 – 8:00 WELCOME TO ALL!

ONE THING THAT ALWAYS SURPRISES ME IS HOW **LITTLE** PARENTS REALLY KNOW ABOUT THEIR CHILDREN'S SCHOOL LIVES!

SURE, YOU CAN ASK THEM "HOW WAS SCHOOL?" BUT WHAT DO YOU REALLY **LEARN?**

THAT'S WHY AN EVENING LIKE THIS CAN BE SO MUCH FUN!

YOU CAN SEE YOUR KIDS' CLASSROOMS! THEIR DESKS! EVEN THEIR **LOCKERS!**

OPENING YOUR CHILD'S LOCKER CAN INTRODUCE YOU TO A KID WHO'S **VERY DIFFERENT** FROM THE ONE YOU SEE AT HOME!

KSSSSSCCH!

...OR A KID WHO'S ALL TOO FAMILIAR.

BiG NATE

by Lincoln Peirce

SPLAT!

YO!

SLIP!

SOMETHING'S NOT RIGHT HERE...

WHAT'S NOT RIGHT?

THIS COMIC STRIP I'M WORKING ON.

IT'S JUST NOT FUNNY! BUT ACCORDING TO ALL THE RULES OF CARTOONING, IT SHOULD BE **HILARIOUS!**

WHAT "RULES OF CARTOONING"?

THERE ARE CERTAIN THINGS THAT ARE SURE-FIRE LAUGH-GETTERS IN COMIC STRIPS! AND I'VE GOT ALL OF 'EM IN HERE!

I'VE GOT A MONKEY, A GUY SLIPPING ON A BANANA PEEL, A TALKING DUCK...

...A FAT GUY IN HIS UNDER-WEAR, A FALLING ANVIL, A HAIRLESS CAT, A GUY GETTING HIT IN THE FACE WITH A PIE...

...AND YET IT'S STILL KIND OF FLAT! I NEED MORE! I'VE GOT TO ADD SOME-THING ELSE!

HOW ABOUT A WEDGIE?

HEY! **YEAH!**

YANK!

THE GALLING THING IS THAT, TECHNICALLY, I GAVE HIM PER-MISSION TO DO THAT.

Peirce

BIG NATE

by Lincoln Peirce

HOME ← SCHOOL →

❋SIGH...❋

WHAT'S WRONG, NATE?

THE **CONTRACT** MY DAD MADE ME SIGN, THAT'S WHAT'S WRONG! IT'S **KILLING** ME!

UNTIL I BRING MY GRADES UP, HE'S NOT LETTING ME DO **ANY-THING!**

NO CLUBS!... NO TEAMS!...NO EXTRA-CURRICULAR ACTIVITIES OF **ANY KIND!**

ALL OF A SUDDEN EVERYONE'S TEAS-ING ME AND SAY-ING I HAVE NO LIFE!

THE WHOLE SCHOOL'S LAUGHING AT ME! THEY CALL ME "STRAIGHT HOME" WRIGHT BECAUSE THAT'S WHERE I GO AFTER SCHOOL: **STRAIGHT HOME!**

WELL, SHAME ON THEM, THEN!

THE NUMBER OF **TEAMS** SOME-ONE'S ON ISN'T THE MEASURE OF A PERSON!

IT'S WHO YOU **ARE** THAT MATTERS, NOT WHAT YOU **DO!**

YOU ARE NOT WHAT YOU DO, NATE! OKAY? YOU ARE **NOT** WHAT YOU DO!

...OR SO I KEEP TELLING MYSELF.

BIG NATE

by Lincoln Peirce

OW! DANG!

AN APPLE FOR THE TEACHER?

YUP!

YOU SHOULD TRY IT! IT WOULDN'T HURT YOU TO GET ON HER GOOD SIDE!

NO, THANKS.

SUIT YOURSELF! I'LL GET ON HER GOOD SIDE!

YOU DO THAT.

MRS. GODFREY?

YES, FRANCIS?

I HAVE A LITTLE SOMETHING FOR YOU!

JUST A LITTLE TOKEN OF MY ESTEEM, THAT'S ALL!

CRUNCH!

THANKS FOR BEING A GREAT TEACHER!

WELL, ISN'T THAT—

!

I'M ASKING THE SCHOOL NURSE FOR A COPY OF YOUR DENTAL RECORDS.

84

BIG NATE

by Lincoln Peirce

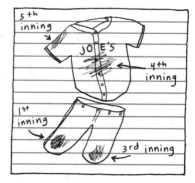

5th inning
JOE'S
4th inning
1st inning
3rd inning

WHAT A GAME!

IT WAS NICE TO ACTUALLY **WIN** ONE!

HMPH! SOME GAME!

I WALKED FOUR TIMES AND DIDN'T GET A SINGLE BALL HIT TO ME IN THE FIELD!

LOOK AT MY UNIFORM! NOT A SINGLE SMUDGE! NOT A SINGLE STAIN!

IF WE RUN INTO ANYONE WE KNOW, THEY'LL THINK I SPENT THE ENTIRE GAME ON THE **BENCH**!

I'VE GOT TO MESS UP MY UNIFORM SO THAT I LOOK LIKE A **BALLPLAYER**!

SPLURCH!

DO YOU THINK I WANT TO WALK AROUND LOOKING LIKE A **LOSER**?

ROLL ROLL

THE EVIDENCE CERTAINLY SUPPORTS THAT, YES.

HEL-LO!

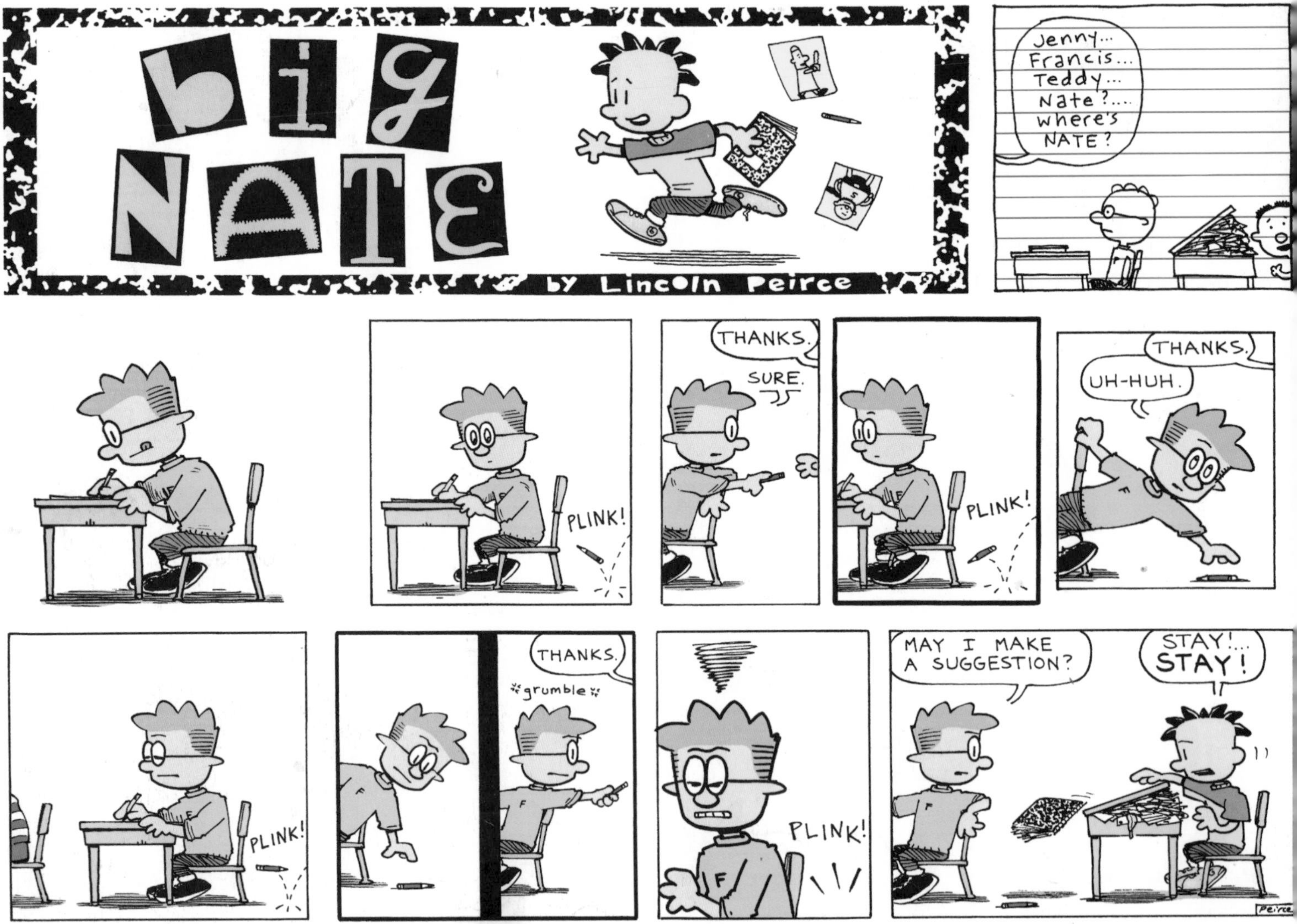
big NATE
by Lincoln Peirce
Jenny... Francis... Teddy... Nate?.... where's NATE?
PLINK!
THANKS.
SURE.
PLINK!
THANKS.
UH-HUH.
PLINK!
THANKS.
grumble
PLINK!
MAY I MAKE A SUGGESTION?
STAY!... STAY!
Peirce

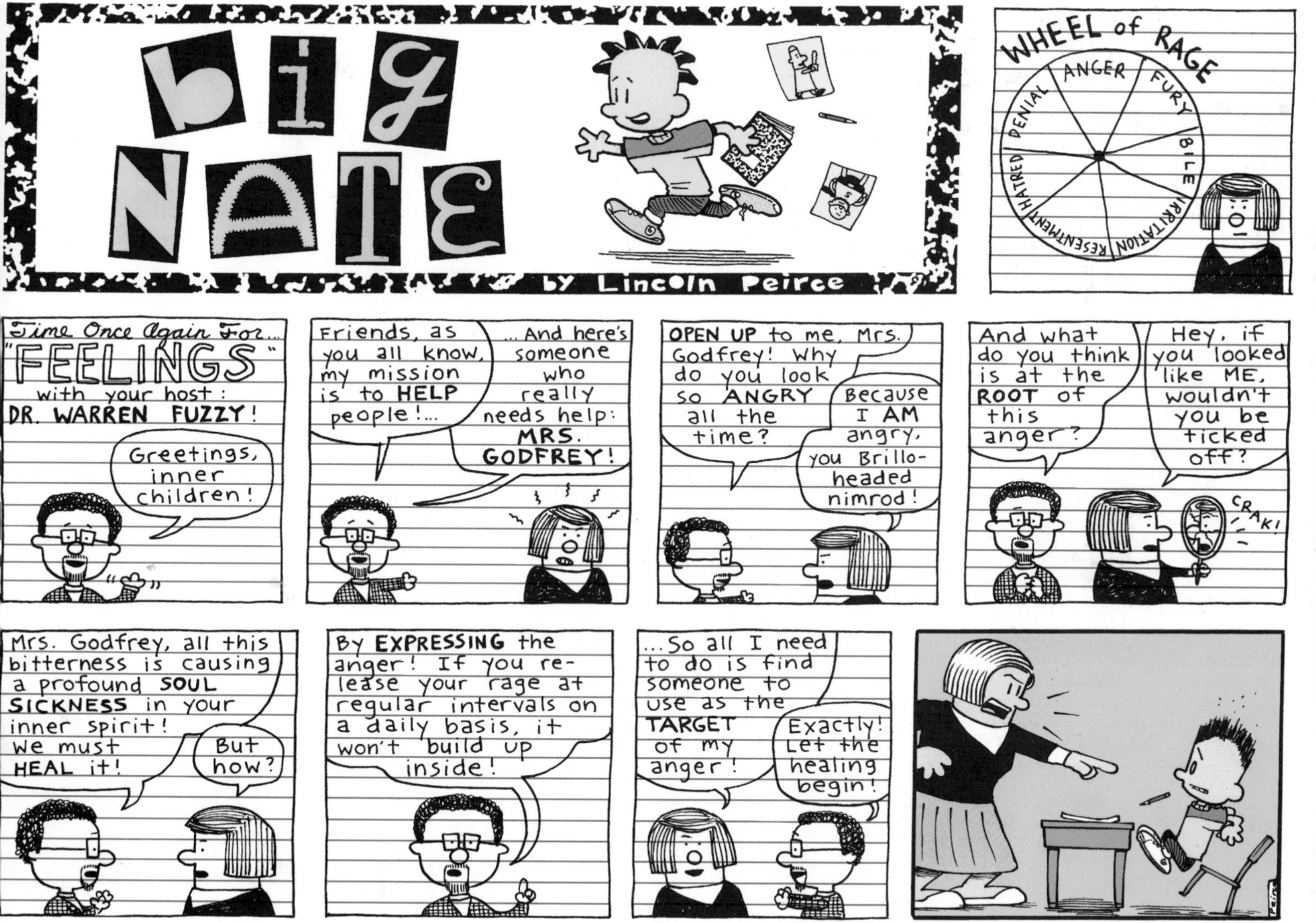
big NATE
by Lincoln Peirce
WHEEL of RAGE
ANGER
FURY
BILE
IRRITATION
RESENTMENT
HATRED
DENIAL
Time Once Again For... "FEELINGS" with your host: DR. WARREN FUZZY!
Greetings, inner children!
Friends, as you all know, my mission is to HELP people!...
...And here's someone who really needs help: MRS. GODFREY!
OPEN UP to me, Mrs. Godfrey! Why do you look so ANGRY all the time?
Because I AM angry, you Brillo-headed nimrod!
And what do you think is at the ROOT of this anger?
Hey, if you looked like ME, wouldn't you be ticked off?
CRAK!
Mrs. Godfrey, all this bitterness is causing a profound SOUL SICKNESS in your inner spirit! We must HEAL it!
But how?
By EXPRESSING the anger! If you release your rage at regular intervals on a daily basis, it won't build up inside!
...So all I need to do is find someone to use as the TARGET of my anger!
Exactly! Let the healing begin!

big NATE

by Lincoln Peirce

Time Once Again For...
★ ★ ★ ★ ★ ★ ★ ★ ★
Celebrity
INTERVIEW!!

with your host:
BIFF BIFFWELL!

Folks, I'm talking to our old friend **HOPSY** the **EASTER BUNNY!** Hopsy, you look **EXHAUSTED!**

I am, Biff.

That's understandable, Hopsy,... after all, you just delivered candy to millions of children throughout the world!

Not just children, Biff!

Huh?

Bringing candy to kids is the **EASY** part of my job!

The thing that **REALLY** wrinkles my cotton is making those gigantic deliveries to **PARENTS!**

You... you bring candy to **PARENTS?**

Well... I'm not supposed to talk about it... but **OF COURSE** I do!

...And I'm not talking just a few jelly beans, either! If the **KIDS** ever saw what their **PARENTS** are getting, we'd have a **RIOT** on our hands!

HEY!

big NATE

by Lincoln Peirce

POP QUIZ, PEOPLE!

POP!

Hello again, friends! Investigative reporter **CHIP CHIPSON** here with another edition of...

TEAC LOU

BEHIND THE SCENES IN THE **TEACHERS' LOUNGE!**

I'm here in the teachers' inner sanctum at P.S. 38, where Social Studies instructor **Mrs. GODFREY** is GRADING TESTS!

Multiple choice, Mrs. G?

Essay tests, Chip.

Why essays? So that you can assess each student's writing skills, expressive capabilities and subject knowledge?

¡Snicker¡ Chip, you're so naive.

Essay tests are simply more **FUN** to grade! Why? Because there aren't any hard-and-fast "right" or "wrong" answers!

That enables me to indulge all my personal feelings about my students while assigning grades! Watch carefully...

Here's **NATE WRIGHT'S** essay! As we all know, I **DESPISE** Nate because his talent and charisma remind me what a miserable human being I am!

So you'll give him a bad grade? Even if his essay is **BRILLIANT?**

Precisely, Chip. Life's not fair. NYA HA HA HA!

D-MINUS?

JUST AN OBSERVATION: HIS FIRST NAME WAS "BENEDICT," NOT "TOM!"

89

BIG NATE

by Lincoln Peirce

GOOD GRAVY! **TIME OUT!**

THIS IS THE LAMEST PRACTICE WE'VE EVER HAD! WHAT'S **WITH** YOU GUYS?

YOU BIG GUYS ARE SUPPOSED TO BE OUR SCORING THREAT! YOU LOOK **PATHETIC** OUT THERE!

WE'RE GOING TO HAVE TO PLAY BETTER THAN THIS AGAINST JEFFERSON TOMORROW!

HOW, YOU ASK? I'LL TELL YOU! **I**, NATE WRIGHT, AM THE **KEY** TO THE GAME!

NONE OF **YOU** GUYS WANT TO TAKE CONTROL OF THIS TEAM, SO **I** WILL! CLIMB ON MY BACK!

YES, **I** WILL LEAD US TO VICTORY! I REPEAT: **CLIMB ON MY BACK!**

SOUNDS GOOD.

C-CAN'T BREATHE...

HEY, GUYS! HOP ON!

BIG NATE by Lincoln Peirce

I'M HANDING BACK YOUR TESTS, PEOPLE!

Time Once Again For... "BIFF AND CHIP." **ON SAFARI!**

G'day, mates!

Today we're on the trail of one of nature's most frightening creatures: the 6th grade social studies teacher!

...Or, as she's known in scientific terms: "BAD BREATHIUS HIDEOSA"!

There's one NOW! Ye Gads, what an ugly beast!

And her disposition matches her appearance, Biff!

Ah! So she's bad-tempered, eh?

Is she EVER! She routinely bites the heads off of her helpless victims!

But how does she catch her victims in the FIRST place?

Simple, Biff! She lulls them to sleep with a nasty little weapon we call... the "LECTURE"!

...And then, after the first Continental Congress in 1774, the colonists decided...

Hmm... NOW what's she doing?

A common practice among her species! She's MARKING her TERRITORY!

With what, Chip?

It appears to be a standard RED FELT-TIP PEN!

big NATE

by Lincoln Peirce

SUGAR PIE

CHATTER CHATTER GIGGLE YAK YAK

OH, **THERE** YOU ARE, SUGAR PIE! I'VE BEEN LOOKING ALL OVER FOR YOU!

ER...I'LL SEE YOU LATER, JENNY.

seethe

LATER, BRAD!

NATE! IN THE FLESH!

WILL YOU **STOP** DOING THAT!

DOING WHAT?

CALLING ME "SUGAR PIE"! I DON'T WANT TO BE CALLED THAT! YOU HAVE **NO RIGHT** TO CALL ME THAT!

HMMM... Y'KNOW, I SEE YOUR POINT...

IT'S NOT FAIR FOR ME TO GIVE **YOU** A PET NAME UNLESS YOU GIVE **ME** ONE!

WHY DON'T YOU CALL ME "CUDDLE BUNS"?

CUDDLE BUNS?!

I CAN'T TAKE IT.

WE'RE AN ITEM!

BIG NATE
by Lincoln Peirce

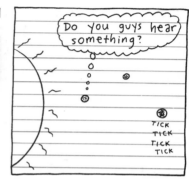

Do you guys hear something?

TICK
TICK
TICK
TICK

CARTOONING CLUB!

WOW!

MEETING TODAY

3:00 ROOM 115

DANG!

WHAT'S THE PROBLEM, TEDDY?

I'VE DRAWN MYSELF INTO A CORNER!

I DREW THE FIRST THREE PANELS OF A COMIC STRIP... AND NOW I DON'T KNOW HOW TO FINISH IT!

WRITER'S BLOCK, EH?

ALLOW **ME**, TEDDY! AS A FUTURE PROFESSIONAL CARTOONIST, I'M AN **EXPERT** AT THIS SORT OF THING!

HUMM DEE DUMM..... I'LL JUST ADD A FOURTH PANEL TO THE THREE YOU DID, AND... **VOILA**! A COMIC **MASTERPIECE**!"

PANEL ONE: GUY WALKS INTO A PET STORE!...

PANEL TWO: GUY ASKS, "GOT ANY GOLDFISH?"

PANEL THREE: SALESMAN REPLIES, "I'M SORRY, SIR. NOT TODAY."

PANEL FOUR: PLANET EARTH, FOR NO APPARENT REASON, EXPLODES IN A FIERY BALL OF FLAME!

KA-BLOOM!

by Lincoln Peirce

Biff Biffwell, "celebrity interviewer," speaks with...

APRIL SHOWERS!!

April, I think our viewers are wondering: what's happened to your usual "SUNNY" disposition?

Well, Biff, lately I...

SAAAAY! Who's THAT?

THAT'S the reason I'm in a bad mood: my obnoxious sister, MAY FLOWERS!

LOOK at her, will you? She thinks she's so great, tossing blossoms all over the place!

But who makes the flowers grow in the FIRST place? ME! I do all the work, SHE hogs all the credit!

Nobody LIKES rain, that's the problem! Nobody appreciates my talents! It's so UNFAIR!

Everyone's always asking, "why can't you be more like your sister?" I'm SICK of it!

ARE YOU TRYING TO MAKE A POINT HERE?

YOU'RE AN ONLY CHILD. YOU DON'T KNOW WHAT I'VE BEEN THROUGH.

94

BIG NATE
by Lincoln Peirce

OOH! OOH! OOH!

TAPPA TAPPA TIPPITY TAP

WHEN DID THE BILL OF RIGHTS GO INTO EFFECT? ANYONE?

OOH! OOH! OOH!

NATE?

POINK!

UMMMM...

OOH! OOH!

OOH! OOH!!

HEY! DO YOU MIND?

I'M ANSWERING THIS ONE, GINA! OR AT LEAST I WILL, ONCE YOU STOP CIRCLING AROUND ME LIKE A VULTURE!

PLENTY OF PEOPLE BESIDES **YOU** ARE CAPABLE OF GETTING A RIGHT ANSWER!

NATE? THE BILL OF RIGHTS WENT INTO EFFECT IN...?

UMM... SEVENTEEN SEVENTY-SIX

OOH!

GINA?

I'M BEGINNING TO SEE THE APPEAL OF HOME SCHOOLING.

BIG NATE

by Lincoln Peirce

"MOM"

Clerk: CAN I HELP YOU?

Nate: I'M LOOKING FOR A MOTHER'S DAY CARD.

Clerk: RIGHT OVER THERE. AISLE TWO.

Nate: I LOOKED AT THOSE ALREADY. I COULDN'T FIND WHAT I WAS LOOKING FOR.

Nate: DON'T YOU HAVE ANY THAT JUST SAY, "HAPPY MOTHER'S DAY, DAD"?

Clerk: "HAPPY MOTHER'S DAY, **DAD**"?

Nate: YEAH.

Clerk: WE DON'T HAVE ANY CARDS LIKE THAT... HOW ABOUT ONE THAT SAYS, "DEAR DAD: SINCE MOM DIVORCED YOU, YOU'VE BEEN A GREAT MOTHER"?

Nate: UH... NO.

Clerk: HOW ABOUT "DAD: OTHER KIDS' MOMS AREN'T HALF THE MAN YOU ARE"?

Nate: SORRY.

BERRY'S STATIONERS
"CARDS FOR ANY OCCASION"

Nate: HA!

big NATE

by Lincoln Peirce

WHAM!

SPITSY! EASY! **DOWN**, BOY!

SLUP
SLUP
SLUP
SLUP

SORRY ABOUT THAT, NATE.

✳ SPLUT! ✳ SPITSY, YOU **IDIOT!** WHAT IS **WITH** YOU?

PANT PANT PANT

WHAT'S WITH HIM? HE **MISSES** YOU, OF COURSE!

YOU TOOK CARE OF HIM ALL LAST WEEK! THE TWO OF YOU **BONDED!**

HE NOW THINKS OF YOU NOT JUST AS THE KID NEXT DOOR, BUT MORE LIKE A **PARENT!**

HAPPY MOTHER'S DAY!

BIG NATE

BY Lincoln Peirce

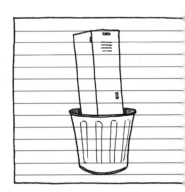

KA CHINK!

KSSSCH!

RRRRUMBLE!...

? ?

RRRUMMBLE!...

FFFFOOOOOOMM!

HI.

IT'S HIS END-OF-THE-YEAR LOCKER CLEANING.

BIG NATE by Lincoln Peirce

Panel 1:
ALL RIGHT, "JOE'S CHICKEN"! LET'S LISTEN UP!

Panel 2:
GUYS, THE SEASON'S NOT GOING WELL! WE'RE A LAUGHING-STOCK BECAUSE OF OUR RIDICULOUS TEAM NAME!

Panel 3:
BUT TODAY WE CAN TURN IT ALL AROUND! WE CAN **BEAT** THIS TEAM AND START TO CHANGE EVERY-ONE'S OPINION OF US!

Panel 4:
BUT TO DO THAT, WE'VE GOT TO FOCUS ON THE BASICS OF **BASEBALL**! PITCHING! HITTING! BASERUNNING! STRATEGY!

Panel 5:
LET'S IGNORE ALL THE LAME JOKES AND WISE-CRACKS AND COME UP WITH A GAME PLAN! HOW ABOUT IT, "JOE'S CHICKEN"?

Panel 6:
I THINK WE SHOULD JUST "WING" IT.

Panel 7:
HEH HEH "WING" IT!... HA HA HA GOOD ONE, MAN! HEE HEE HA HA

Panel 8:
HA HA HA HA HA HA HA HA HA HA HA HA

WE HEREBY FORFEIT DUE TO A LACK OF SELF-RESPECT.

by Lincoln Peirce

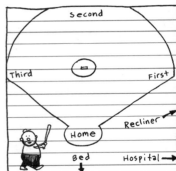

Second

Third

First

Recliner

Home

Bed   Hospital →

HEY HEY HEY!

WANNA PLAY SOME CATCH?

SURE! I'LL GET MY GLOVE!

FINALLY IT'S REALLY STARTING TO FEEL LIKE SPRING!

THIS IS JUST THE SORT OF WEATHER THAT GETS ME PUMPED FOR BASEBALL!

THE SMELL OF THE GRASS... THE FEEL OF THE GLOVE...

THE ROAR OF THE CROWD...

THE CRACK OF THE BACK...

OF THE BAT, YOU MEAN.

NOPE. LOOK.

OH.

LAST YEAR, HE WAS IN TRACTION FOR TWO WEEKS.

BIG NATE

by Lincoln Peirce

Hey, TRIVIA LOVERS!!

Test your knowledge of everyone's favorite bleached-blonde high school sophomore!

⟨?⟩⟨?⟩⟨?⟩⟨?⟩⟨?⟩⟨?⟩⟨?⟩

TAKE THE Ellen Wright

FUN FACTS QUIZ!

QUESTION 1: Ellen's IQ is less than that of:

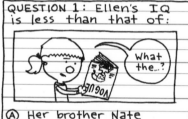

- (A) Her brother Nate
- (B) A sickly kitten
- (C) A potato
- (D) All of the above

Question 2: Ellen's boyfriend Gordie is:

- (A) A gentleman
- (B) A scholar
- (C) Woefully misguided
- (D) Insane

QUESTION 3: Ellen's hobbies include:

- (A) Mustache-bleaching
- (B) Quantum astrophysics
- (C) Sobbing in front of mirror
- (D) A and C

QUESTION 4: Ellen's reason for living is:

Move. *SHOVE!* *Oh, Billy...*

- (A) Promoting world peace
- (B) Ending poverty
- (C) Achieving enlightenment
- (D) "Melrose Place"

Question 5: Which "clique" does Ellen belong to at school?

Hi, gang! *Who are you?*

- (A) The "Preps"
- (B) The "Brains"
- (C) The "Jocks"
- (D) The "Friendless Losers"

GREAT JOB!

To find out the correct answers, turn the page **UPSIDE-DOWN!**

D, D, D, D, D

BIG NATE

by Lincoln Peirce

BOOOOOOO! BOOOOOO!

HEY, GUYS!

WHA—? ※SPUTTER!※...WHAT IS THAT **CAT** DOING HERE?

PICKLES IS GOING TO BE OUR MASCOT! AREN'T YOU, GIRL?

NO **WAY!** I DON'T WANT ANY **CAT** ON OUR TEAM!

OH, I FORGOT! YOU'RE **AFRAID** OF CATS!

I AM **NOT!** I JUST DON'T **LIKE** 'EM, THAT'S ALL!

BUT CATS ARE **GOOD LUCK!** EVERYBODY KNOWS THAT!

GOOD LUCK? NOT TO **ME!**

BESIDES, WHAT DOES **LUCK** HAVE TO DO WITH ANYTHING? BASEBALL IS A GAME OF **SKILL!**

NOW KEEP THAT CAT OUT OF MY WAY SO I CAN BAT!

FWIP!

meow!

YAAA!

BACK! BACK, YOU VILE FELINE!

GOOD LUCK OR NOT, LET'S KEEP HER AROUND FOR THE ENTERTAINMENT VALUE!

BIG NATE

by Lincoln Peirce

Panel 1

SO JENNY'S GOING STEADY WITH RONNIE DWYER! POOR NATE MUST BE **DEVASTATED!**

HE'LL LIVE

Panel 2

WHAT KIND OF ATTITUDE IS **THAT**, FRANCIS? NATE NEEDS OUR **SUPPORT!** HE'S PROBABLY REALLY HURTING!

I'M GONNA TALK TO HIM!

Panel 3

NATE? I... UH... I HEARD ABOUT JENNY AND RONNIE, AND... WELL, I JUST WANT TO SAY: I'M HERE FOR YOU!

Panel 4

I MEAN... THERE MUST BE A LOT GOING ON INSIDE YOU!... EATING AWAY AT YOU!

Panel 5

DON'T YOU THINK YOU'D FEEL BETTER IF YOU JUST... LET IT OUT?

LET WHAT OUT?

Panel 6

WHATEVER YOU'RE FEELING! DON'T THINK ABOUT IT! JUST LET IT OUT!

LET IT OUT. WELL... OKAY

Panel 7

BURRP!

Panel 8

HE'LL LIVE

YOU KNOW, I **DO** FEEL BETTER!

by Lincoln Peirce

GO DIRECTLY TO SCHOOL

DO NOT PASS GO · DO NOT COLLECT $200

"You Just **CAN'T** Win!" IT'S

SCHOOL

THE BOARD GAME!

START →

Locker is declared public health hazard!

SHOOSH! · YAAAAH!

GO TO Detention!

School Cafeteria celebrates "Our Friend the Beet" week!

Eat hearty.

Lose five points!

Substitute gym teacher is ex-marine!

26... 27... 28... Keep that @#!✱ butt **DOWN!**

You WORM!

USMC

Break ankle, lose turn!

Teacher decides to torment you for **NO APPARENT REASON!**

I don't like you, Nate. Go to detention.

You ride the bus with Sheldon ("Odor") O'Daire!

Sardine?

Move back 6 spaces!

You get back brutally hard math test!

POINK!

Lose TEN points!

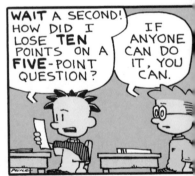

WAIT A SECOND! HOW DID I LOSE **TEN** POINTS ON A **FIVE**-POINT QUESTION?

IF ANYONE CAN DO IT, YOU CAN.

by Lincoln Peirce

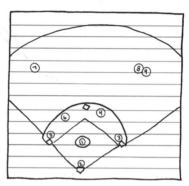

I GOT IT!

I GOT IT!

MINE!

MINE, I SAID!

NO, MINE!

THE **CENTER FIELDER** HAS THE RIGHT OF WAY!

NOT WHEN IT'S HIT TO THE **RIGHT FIELDER!**

IT'S **BETWEEN** US, FOOL!

I CALLED IT **FIRST**, BALL HOG!

SHOVE!

BALL HOG? TAKE THAT BACK!

MAKE ME!

WUMP!

COACH

105

big NATE by Lincoln Peirce

Hey! You're a beautiful crowd! I MEAN that!

Here's a li'l tune called: "The Alien & Sedition Acts of 1798"

OH, HOW I HATE SOCIAL STUDIES. THIS FINAL EXAM IS GOING TO BE **BRUTAL**!

YOU'VE GOT TO FIND WAYS TO MAKE STUDYING **FUN**!

"FUN." RIGHT.

DO WHAT **I** DO! MAKE UP LITTLE POEMS ABOUT THE STUFF YOU'RE STUDYING!

LIKE THIS: "LEWIS AND CLARK IN 1804 WENT WAY OUT WEST TO CHART AND EXPLORE"!

HERE'S ANOTHER ONE: "ROBERT FULTON HAD A DREAM: TO SAIL A SHIP THAT RAN ON STEAM"!

HEY, THAT'S PRETTY GOOD!

AND IT **WORKS**, TOO! IT REALLY HELPS YOU REMEMBER THE STUFF!

✶CHUCKLE!✶ I COULDN'T HELP OVERHEARING! THAT'S A GOOD IDEA, FRANCIS!

...BUT YOU KNOW WHAT MIGHT WORK EVEN **BETTER**? SETTING THOSE POEMS TO **MUSIC**!

JOIN IN, BOYS!

PLINK PL NK

MAKING UP POEMS GOOD ONE BUDDY.

LET'S FIND SOMEWHERE ELSE TO STUDY.

BIG NATE

by Lincoln Peirce

"END O' SCHOOL" (a poem)

by Nate Wright

September brought us back to school,
A situation downright cruel.
And by October, we'd recalled,
Why by our school we're so appalled.

Here's tonight's homework.

Did I mention that homework counts for 80% of your grade?

GROOANNN

Dang!

November: time for Giving thanks.
I tried, but kept on Drawing blanks.

Thank goodness you didn't get an F-MINUS!

Shut up, man.

We reached December,
Inch by inch.
That Mrs. Godfrey:
What a grinch.

Our January resolution:
Start a 6th-grade revolution!

FOOD FIGHT!

February's short,
You mention?
Not if you spend it
In detention.

Sigh...

tick tick tick

March and April came and went.
Can't we give up school for Lent?
May and June: we got exam'd.
I failed despite how much I crammed.

Ready for your test on Chapter six?

But you told us to study Chapter FIVE!!

I changed my mind.

Now finally it's Really summer!
School's out! Let's get..

"DUMB AND DUMBER"?

NAH. HOW 'BOUT "MEN IN BLACK"?

BY Lincoln Peirce

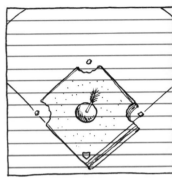

TIE GAME...

BOTTOM OF THE NINTH...

TWO OUTS...

BASES LOADED...

YES, IT'S DEFINITELY "CRUNCH" TIME!

CRUNCH!

OUR NEW RIGHT FIELDER IS EATING CHIPS.

COACH

BIG NATE

by Lincoln Peirce

BEEP
BEEP
BOOP
BEEP
BEEP
BOOP
BOOP

busy signal

BEEP
BEEP
BOOP
BEEP
BEEP
BOOP
BOOP

busy signal   busy signal

YAWNN

BEEP
BEEP
BOOP
BEEP
BEEP
BOOP
BOOP

busy signal

BEEP
BEEP
BOOP
BEEP
BEEP
BOOP
BOOP

RRRINNNG!

WKQC-FM! YOU'RE THE HUNDREDTH CALLER! WANT TO WIN A HUNDRED DOLLARS?

YES! YES!

OKAY, JUST ANSWER THIS QUESTION: WHO WAS FRANKLIN ROOSEVELT'S **FIRST** VICE PRESIDENT?

KLIK

THE "REDIAL" BUTTON CAN TAKE YOU TO THE STATION, BUT IT CAN'T GET YOU ON THE TRAIN.

"UP CLOSE AND PERSONAL"

with your host: **CHIP CHIPSON!**

Hello again, friends! My special guest today: consumer reporter **CELINE PAYCHEK!**

Hi, Chip!

Celine, at this time of year, kids everywhere are wondering: WHAT can I get Dad for **FATHER'S DAY??**

I can help, Chip!

I've got plenty of gift ideas for the Dad who has everything!

For example: the **NOSTRIL PILOT,®** a handy little nose-hair trimmer!

BZZZZZZ

BEFORE

Or how about the **PANTS-HORN®** to help Dad into those slacks that have gotten ☆chuckle!☆ a bit snug!

HERE'S a handy little item! An edible couch! No more pesky trips to the fridge during that big game!

AND it comes in chocolate, beef, and monterey jack!

YUM!

But Celine... what if a kid spent all his money on candy and video games, and can't **AFFORD** one of these gifts?

No problem at all, Chip!

Just dust off the ol' "it's the thought that counts" excuse! Give Dad something **HOMEMADE,** like a lame DRAWING you were planning to throw away **ANYWAY!** He'll **LOVE** it!

I LOVE IT!

☆PHEW!☆

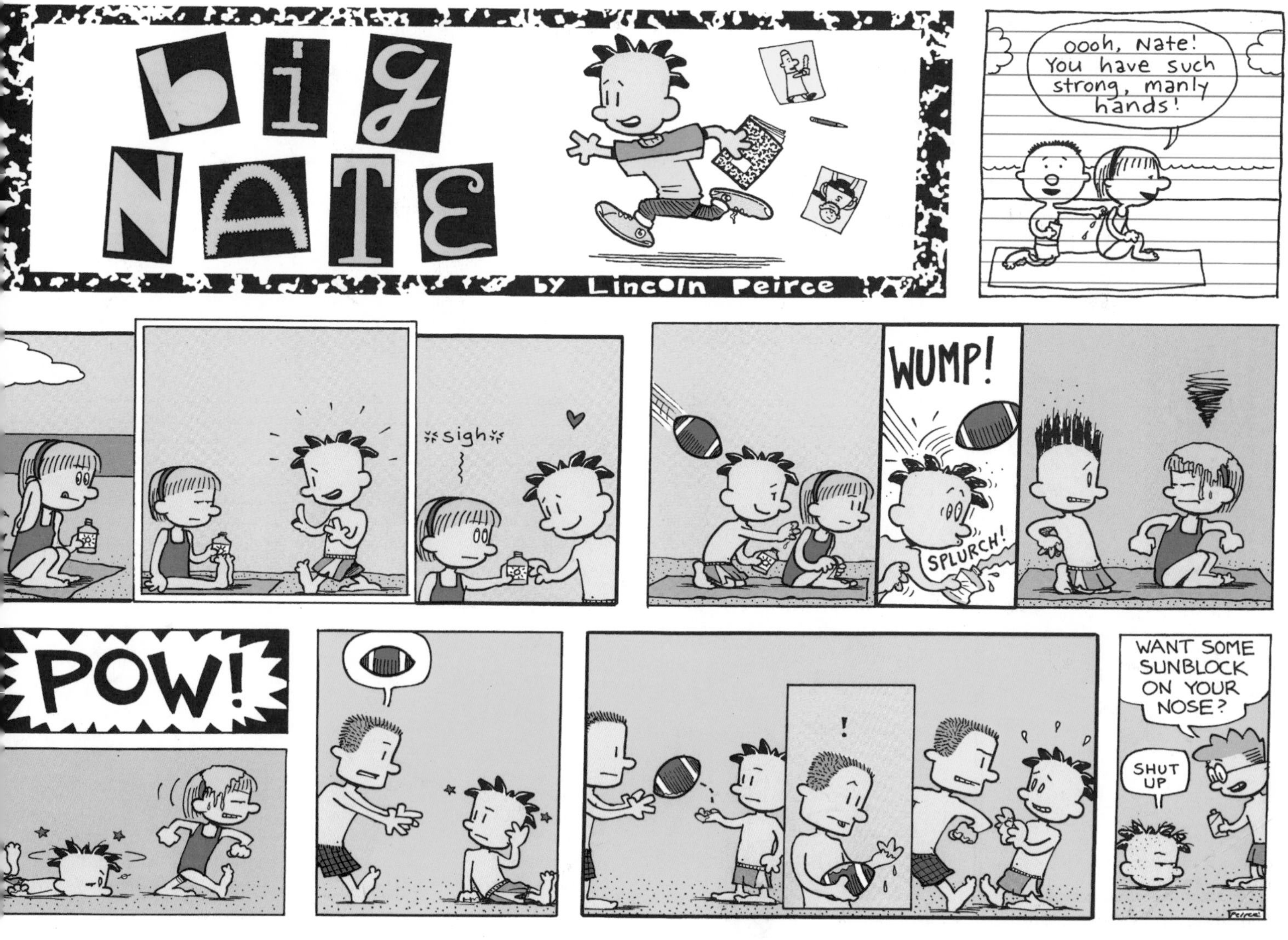

big NATE
by Lincoln Peirce
oooh, Nate! You have such strong, manly hands!
sigh
WUMP!
SPLURCH!
POW!
!
WANT SOME SUNBLOCK ON YOUR NOSE?
SHUT UP

by Lincoln Peirce

The SOUNDS of BASE-BALL

SCUFF
SCUFF

TAP TAP

grunt!

KRAK!

CLAP CLAP
CLAP CLAP
CLAP

YAWNNNN

ding ding ♪♫

THUMP!

ICE

WAP!

COACH

big NATE

by Lincoln Peirce

IN HONOR OF "CARTOON APPRECIATION WEEK," I'M GOING TO DO A LITTLE DEMONSTRATION!

I'LL START OFF WITH A SIMPLE DRAWING OF MY SISTER ELLEN!

NOW OBSERVE AS I USE A FEW CARTOONING TRICKS TO COMPLETELY CHANGE HER APPEARANCE!

FIRST I'LL ADD SOME EYEBROWS AND TEETH...

NEXT, I'LL MAKE HER FACE ALL FLUSHED...

...AND I'LL ADD STEAM COMING OUT OF HER EARS!

SWEAT BEADS ARE GOOD! AND I'LL CHANGE HER EYES A BIT!

HOW 'BOUT HER EYES SHOOTING DAGGERS?

AND... **UH OH!** SHE'S THINKING NASTY THOUGHTS!

SEE HOW EASY IT IS TO MAKE HER MAD?

GOOD THING IT'S JUST A CARTOON!

BIG NATE

by Lincoln Peirce

♡ Oh, Nate! Seeing you hit that home run off my current boyfriend Ronnie has made me change my mind and fall madly in love with YOU! ♡

KRAK!

voice of Jenny →

WELL, WELL, **WELL!** LOOK WHO'S **PITCHING!**

RONNIE DWYER! THE ALL-AMERICAN BOY!

WHAT DOES JENNY **SEE** IN THIS GUY? HE'S SUCH A **JERK!**

BALL ONE!

BALL TWO!

BALL THREE!

HA! NOT ONLY IS HE A JERK, HE'S **AFRAID** OF ME! HE'S PITCHING **AROUND** ME!

WHATSA MATTER, RONNIE? AFRAID I'M GONNA PUT ONE OVER THE FENCE??

GIMME ALL YOU GOT, WIMP! COME ON! COME RIGHT AT ME!

WUMP!

WAS THAT REALLY CALLED FOR?

PRETTY MUCH WORD FOR WORD.

big NATE

by Lincoln Peirce

"Pull Up A Desk!"
TIME once AGAIN for....
Dan Cupid's LOVE SEMINAR!

Lecture Hall

Recruits, I'm here to tell you that being a matchmaker isn't all flowers and valentines! It can be a tough business!

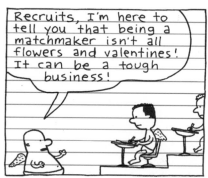

Take **THIS** time of year, for instance! We're coming face-to-face with the phenomenon called "**SUMMER LOVIN'**"!

Travolta   New John

"What's wrong with summer romance?" you ask? **EVERYTHING**!! It wipes out all of **OUR** hard work!

All year long we bust our humps bringing people together! We TIRE-LESSLY pair folks up and help them get through the long, cold winter!

But then **SUMMER** comes along! People get crazy! Blood runs hot!

Before you know it, some mindless summer flirtation can destroy the romances that **WE** worked so hard to create!

AHEM!   HI

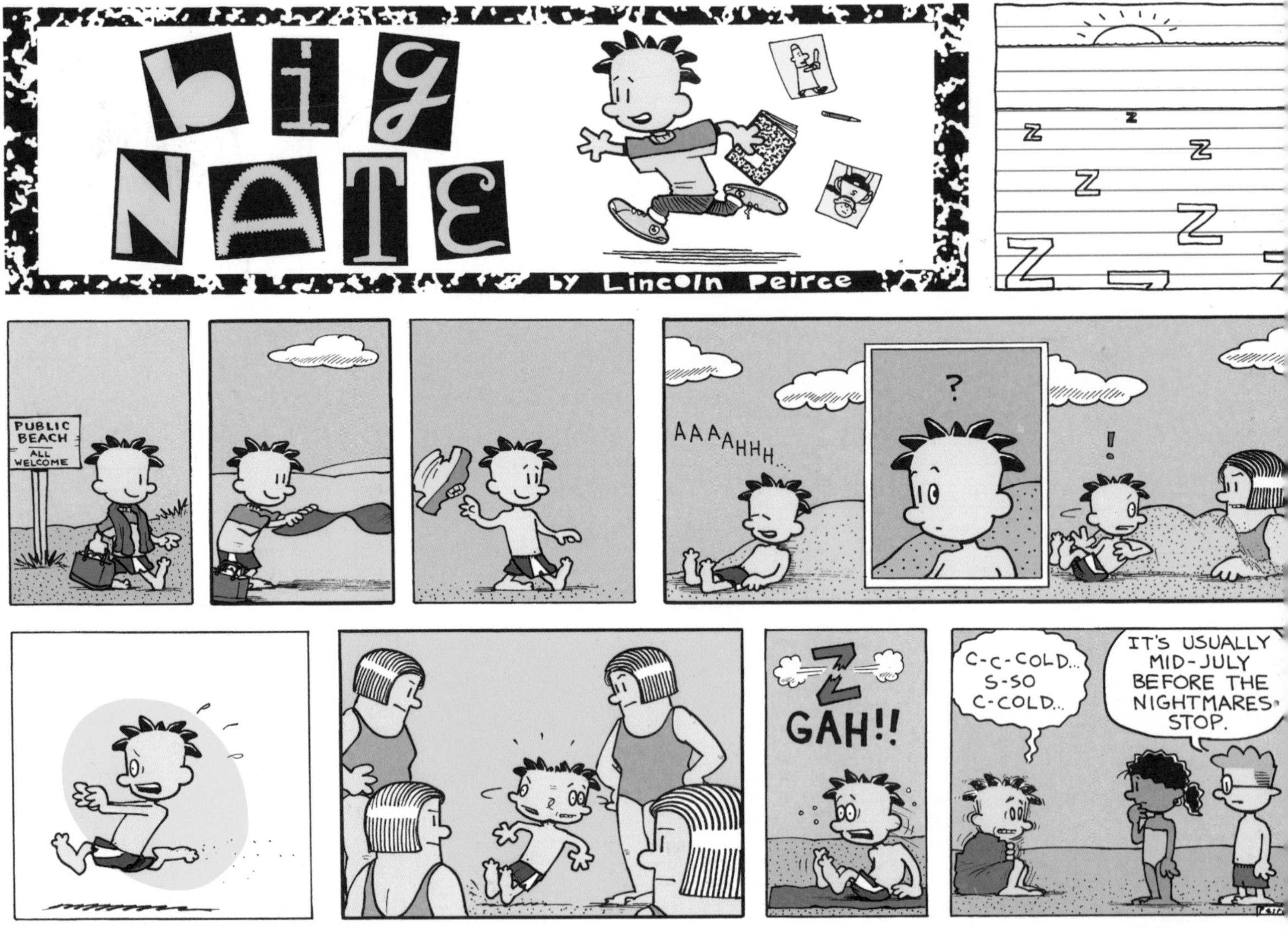
big NATE
by Lincoln Peirce
Z Z Z Z Z
PUBLIC BEACH
ALL WELCOME
AAAAHHH...
?
!
GAH!!
C-C-COLD... S-SO C-COLD...
IT'S USUALLY MID-JULY BEFORE THE NIGHTMARES STOP.

BIG NATE

by Lincoln Peirce

Time For Another Edition Of...

UP CLOSE AND PERSONAL!

"with your host: **RIFF BIFFWELL!**"

Greetings, friends! Since today is Independence Day, it's a very appropriate time to chat with everyone's favorite relative... **UNCLE SAM!**

Yo, Biff. What it is!

Many folks probably don't know that the name "Uncle Sam" is an extension of the initials **U.S.!**

Righto, Biff! I'm one patriotic dude!

And RECOGNIZABLE, too! **EVERYONE** knows Uncle Sam!

Hey, when you dress like this, you can't be anonymous!

So you like the attention, then?

Oh, yeah! What's not to like?

Especially **TODAY!** The 4TH of July is the highlight of my entire **YEAR!**

It's a great feeling to know that at picnics and parades all over the country, people are going to be paying tribute to me however they can!

HEY, JENNY! "I WANT YOU"! HA HA! GET IT?

⚡SIGH...⚡

4TH OF JU
SCOUT TRO

big NATE

WILBURN CHESS CAMP

NO TRESPASSING

ANOTHER MATCH?

NO, LET'S PLAY THE "SCRIBBLE GAME". I NEED TO THINK ABOUT SOMETHING BESIDES CHESS!

I ♥ CHESS

WHAT'S THE "SCRIBBLE GAME"?

I CLOSE MY EYES AND MAKE A QUICK SCRIBBLE, SEE...

I ♥ CHESS

THEN YOU HAVE TO TURN IT INTO SOMETHING!

THAT'S EASY! IT'S A CHESS BOARD!

draw draw

OKAY, THEN...TRY **THIS** ONE!

scribble scribble

THIS ONE'S OBVIOUS! IT'S A KNIGHT CAPTURING A ROOK!

draw draw

ALL RIGHT, DEREK... GET A LOAD OF **THIS** ONE!

scribble scrawl

LOOKS LIKE A DUCK PLAYING CHESS!

NO! **NO!** IT'S **NOT** A DUCK PLAYING CHESS! NOT **EVERY-THING** IS ABOUT **CHESS!**

I ♥ CHESS

YOU! KID! DOES THIS SCRIBBLE LOOK LIKE A DUCK PLAYING CHESS?

A DUCK PLAYING CHESS? NO...

CHESS CAMP

IT'S A **MONKEY** PLAYING CHESS!

OOOH! YOU'RE **RIGHT!**

THEY'R SCARIN ME.

I ♥

118

BIG NATE

BY LINCOLN PEIRCE

hands tied behind back

blindfolded

YOWZA!

CHECK-MATE!

HI, NATE!

HE CAN'T SPEAK TO YOU, DEREK.

YOUR BLABBERMOUTH PAL HERE WAS **YAKKING** SO MUCH, I MADE HIM PROMISE TO SHUT UP FOR THE REST OF THE MATCH!

WITHOUT THE ANNOYING SOUND OF HIS VOICE, I CAN CONCENTRATE ON **DESTROYING** HIM!

S I L E N C E

HA! **CHECK!** WHAT DO YOU SAY TO **THAT**, BIG MOUTH?

whisper whisper

HE SAYS "CHECKMATE."

WHA-? **WHAT?!**

HE ALSO SAYS "IN YOUR FACE."

BIG NATE by Lincoln Peirce

SURE YOU WANT TO DO THAT?

OH, NO YOU DON'T, NATE! **NO YOU DON'T!**

WHAT?

YOU'RE TRYING TO GET ME TO TAKE BACK THAT MOVE!

I'VE GOT YOU ON THE ROPES, SO YOU'RE TRYING TO SOW THE SEEDS OF DOUBT IN MY MIND!

YOU ASK "SURE YOU WANT TO DO THAT?"... AS IF YOU'RE TRYING TO BE **HELPFUL!** HA!

WELL, I'VE BEEN PLAYING AGAINST YOU FOR **THREE WEEKS** NOW, NATE! I KNOW ALL YOUR TRICKS!

SO YES! **YES,** I'M SURE I WANT TO DO THAT!

CHECKMATE.

BUT... I THOUGHT YOU WERE USING REVERSE PSYCHOLOGY!

I WAS!

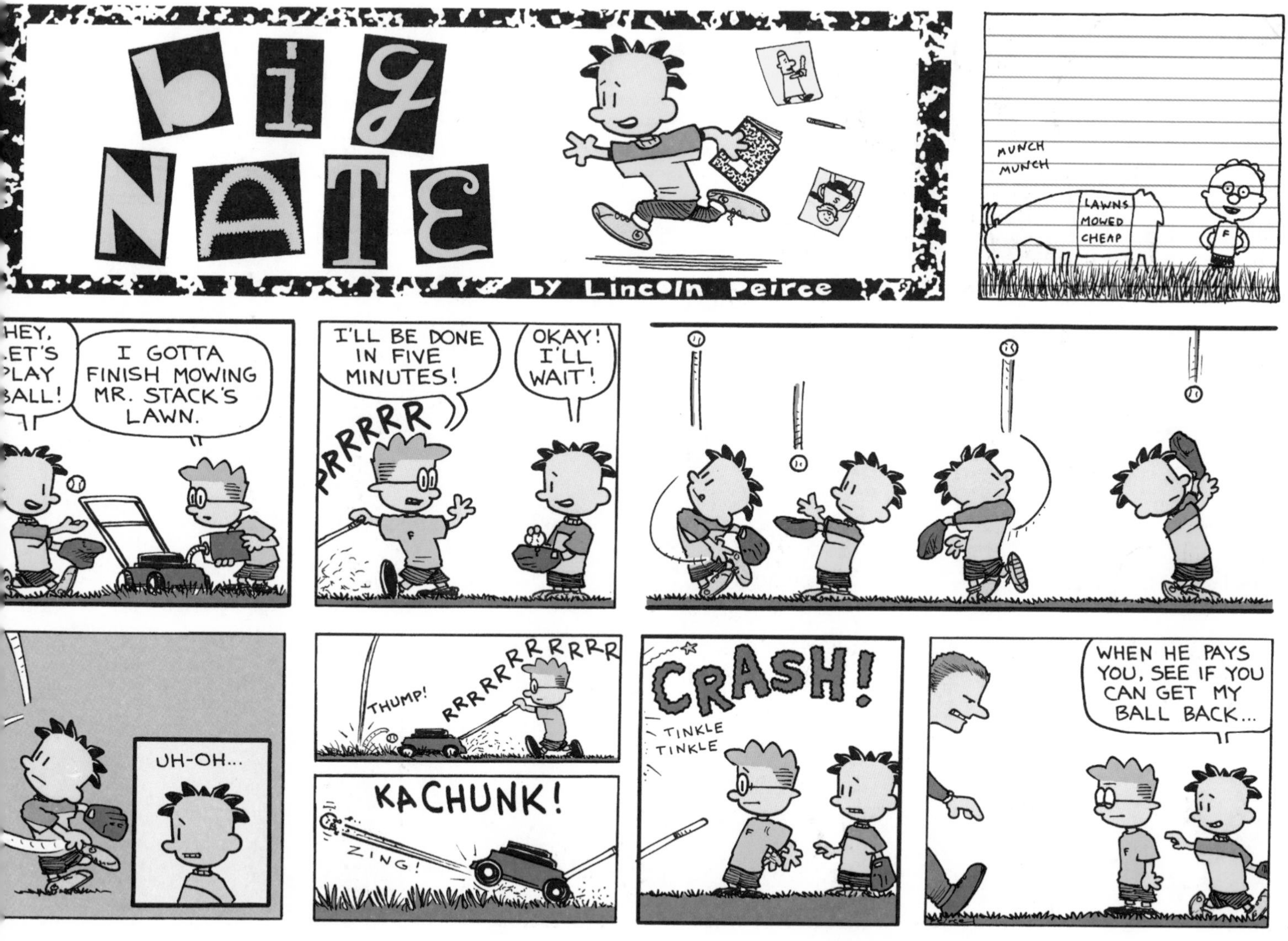
big NATE
by Lincoln Peirce
MUNCH
MUNCH
LAWNS MOWED CHEAP
HEY, LET'S PLAY BALL!
I GOTTA FINISH MOWING MR. STACK'S LAWN.
I'LL BE DONE IN FIVE MINUTES!
RRRRRR
OKAY! I'LL WAIT!
UH-OH...
THUMP!
RRRRRRRRRRR
KACHUNK!
ZING!
CRASH!
TINKLE
TINKLE
WHEN HE PAYS YOU, SEE IF YOU CAN GET MY BALL BACK...

big NATE by Lincoln Peirce

"N.F.T." YARD CARE!

Nate   Francis   Teddy

MOW   MONEY

LET ME HANDLE THIS ONE!

DING DONG!

HI, MA'AM! I COULDN'T HELP NOTICING THAT YOUR LAWN NEEDS MOWING!

MY FRIENDS OVER THERE AND I HAVE A THRIVING LAWN CARE BUSINESS! MOWING, RAKING... WHATEVER!

IF YOU'D LIKE YOUR LAWN TO BE THE ENVY OF THE NEIGHBORHOOD, WE'RE YOUR MEN!

HERE'S OUR CARD! N.F.T. YARD CARE! REMEMBER THE NAME!

!! N.F.T. YARD CARE?

YOU'VE HEARD OF US, EH?

WHO HASN'T?

SLAM!

THE WHOLE "WORD OF MOUTH" THING MAY HAVE STARTED TO BOOMERANG ON US.

BIG NATE by Lincoln Peirce

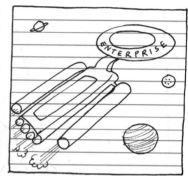

ENTERPRISE

GORDIE! WHAT'S WITH THE BIG MESS!?

INVENTORY! I'VE GOT TO ACCOUNT FOR EVERY ITEM IN THE STORE!

WHA-?... HEY, WHAT'S **THIS** DOING IN A **GARBAGE CAN**?

HM?... OH, WE'RE THROWING THAT OUT. YOU CAN TAKE IT IF YOU WANT.

REALLY?

IT'S ALL YOURS.

TEDDY!

CHECK OUT WHAT THEY WERE THROWING AWAY AT "KLASSIC KOMIX"!

WOW! CAPTAIN PICARD! HOW'D YOU -?

KRAK!

BIFF!

"HEADS UP"!

ALAS, POOR JEAN-LUC.

by Lincoln Peirce

NATE! IS THAT YOUR DOG?

WHO, **SPITSY**? HECK, **NO**! HE'S MY NEIGHBOR'S!

DO YOU HONESTLY THINK I'D OWN A DUMB DOG LIKE **THIS**? HE'D CHEW HIS OWN **PAWS** OFF IF YOU LET HIM!

THAT'S WHY HE WEARS THIS IDIOTIC **COLLAR**! TO PROTECT HIM FROM HIMSELF!

I MEAN, **LOOK** AT HIM IN THAT THING! HE LOOKS LIKE A **CLOWN**!

IF I WERE A DOG, I'D BE **EMBARRASSED** TO BE SEEN IN A COLLAR LIKE—

YANK!

OOF! OW! GAK!

by Lincoln Peirce

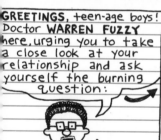

GREETINGS, teen-age boys! Doctor **WARREN FUZZY** here, urging you to take a close look at your relationship and ask yourself the burning question:

WHO WEARS the PANTS: HER or ME??

Select the response that most applies to **YOU**!

① During TV time with my girlfriend, we usually end up watching:

Richard! How COULD you?

SOB!

Ⓐ Something I like
Ⓑ Something we both like
Ⓒ "Caroline In The City"

② Some nights I wake up screaming because I was dreaming about:

YAIEE! NO! **NO!**

Ⓐ drowning in quicksand
Ⓑ falling off a cliff
Ⓒ my girlfriend going public with the fact that she calls me "pookie bear"

③ When I take my girl-friend to a restaurant, I order:

Ooh! That looks yummy!

Ⓐ whatever I want
Ⓑ what I can afford
Ⓒ whatever my girlfriend suggests, then let her eat off my plate

④ My most frequently-worn item of clothing is:

Ⓐ my letterman's jacket
Ⓑ my favorite jeans
Ⓒ a lavender cardigan my girlfriend gave me for our 3½-month anniversary

⑤ When I pick up my girlfriend for a date, I bring with me:

sigh...

tick tick tick

Ⓐ flowers
Ⓑ candy
Ⓒ a magazine to read while waiting for her to get ready

HOW LONG DOES IT TAKE JUST TO PUT ON A DRESS?

ACTUALLY, I THINK SHE'S WEARING THE PANTS.

125

big NATE

by Lincoln Peirce

WHO ARE WE PLAYING TODAY?

THE BULL-DOGS.

YYYESSS! THE BULLDOGS **STINK**! THEY'RE THE ONLY TEAM IN THE LEAGUE WITH A WORSE RECORD THAN **OURS**!

FOR ONCE, WHEN "JOE'S CHICKEN" TAKES THE FIELD, **WE'LL** BE THE FAVORED TEAM!

FOR ONCE, WE WON'T HAVE TO LISTEN TO THE OTHER TEAM **LAUGHING** AT US! THEY'LL KNOW THAT **WE** ARE A BETTER TEAM THAN **THEY** ARE!

I'VE ALMOST FORGOTTEN WHAT IT'S LIKE TO SEE **FEAR** IN AN OPPONENT'S EYES!

HEY, GUYS! LOOK WHO'S HERE!

IT'S "JOE'S CHICKEN"!

CLUCK! CLUCK!

HEH HEH!
BUCK BUCK
BUH-**GAWK**!
HA HA HA HA HA
CLUCK CLUCK BUCK
BUH-**GAW**!

BUCK HA HA
BUCK
HEE HEE
BUH-**GAWK**!
CLUCK HA BUCK BUCK
CLUCK

CLUCK CLUCK
HA HA HA HA

I'VE COM**PLETELY** FORGOTTEN.

BiG NATE

by Lincoln Peirce

CHOMP!

HEY, HEY! LET'S HIT THE ARCADE!

WHAT'S THAT FOR?

THIS IS MY **CARTOONIST'S NOTEBOOK**! I TAKE IT WITH ME WHEREVER I GO!

WHY, YOU ASK? SO WHEN I SEE SOMETHING FUNNY HAPPEN, I CAN QUICKLY WRITE IT DOWN TO USE LATER IN A CARTOON!

THERE'S NOTHING A CARTOONIST HATES MORE THAN FORGETTING A GOOD IDEA! THIS WAY, I FORGET **NOTHING**!

NYAAAAA

WO WO WO

bump
bump
bump
bump

GAAAAA

TONK!

KRRRIP

SPLAT!

WANT ME TO WRITE THAT DOWN FOR YOU?

FORGET IT.

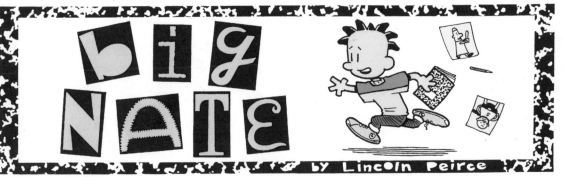

by Lincoln Peirce

"FEELINGS" with your host: DOCTOR WARREN FUZZY!

Let's COMMUNICATE!

Friends, today I'll focus on the INNER LIFE of a TYPICAL TEEN!

...Say! Here's one NOW!

It's ELLEN WRIGHT, fifteen years old and sharp as a sack of wet sand!

B O N K!

...But isn't it true, Ellen, that your vapid and self-absorbed EXTERIOR masks a complex INNER existence?

Is "vapid" good or bad?

What I mean is... your frequent trips to the mall and obsession with the "Backstreet Boys" CAN'T be enough to nourish your SPIRIT!

I don't understand you 'cuz you're using such big words.

I'm asking you to describe your hopes... your dreams... your fears! Show us the REAL Ellen Wright!

Um... should I go freshen up, then?

For Heaven's sake, NO! Just tell us: WHAT IS ELLEN WRIGHT ABOUT??

SHE'S ABOUT TWO FEET BEHIND YOU.

big NATE
by Lincoln Peirce

STEAL
COACH

BALL FOUR!

OKAY, HERE WE GO! RALLY TIME! LATE INNING LIGHTNING!

LET'S SEE WHAT SIGNS COACH IS GIVING ME... HMMMM...

TWO TUGS AT HIS CAP... TWO TAPS ON HIS ARM...

WAIT A SEC... THAT WAS **THREE** TAPS... IS THAT THE "STEAL" SIGN?... HMM...

TWO HANDS ON HIS HIPS... ONE... NO, **TWO** CLAPS...

OW ANOTHER CLAP... AND TWO APS ON HIS SHOULDER... HAT DOES **THAT** MEAN?... HREE TAPS... TWO TUGS...

FOUR CLAPS... TWO SCRATCHES... THREE WHISTLES... ONE... TWO AAARRRGH!

SMAK!

Yer OUT!

TAG!

OKAY, HOW MANY FINGERS?

SHUT UP.

big NATE

by Lincoln Peirce

JENNY! I GOT YOU A TREAT FROM THE SNACK BAR!

WHO ASKED YOU TO GET ME A TREAT?

NOBODY! I WAS JUST BEING NICE!

WELL, I'M NOT EVEN HUNGRY, SO WHY—

HEADS UP!

ZING!

SLUP!

YOW! DID YOU SEE THAT, JENNY? THAT FRISBEE ALMOST—

NYAA!

WHAT? WHAT'S WRONG?

YOU DROPPED IT DOWN MY BACK!!

IT'S FREEZING! IT'S FREEZ-ING!!

I'LL GET IT! I'LL GET IT!

WHAT ARE YOU DOING? GET YOUR HANDS OUT OF MY SUIT!

I'M... I'M JUST... I WAS ONLY...

POW!

I HAVE A POPSICLE HEADACHE.

big NATE

by Lincoln Peirce

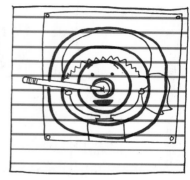

Time For...
Biff and
Chip...

ON SAFARI!

G'day, mates!

Friends, we're here in suburbia to hunt for... the **TEEN-AGER** in her natural habitat!

Her scientific name is "BLEACHED BLONDIUS SELF-ABSORBIA"!

E-GADS, Biff! There she is!!

wipe wipe
spritz spritz
puff puff

What on Earth is she doing, Chip?

It's a bizarre grooming ritual, Biff! It's called "applying makeup"!

KLIK KLIK

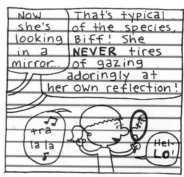

Now she's looking in a mirror...

That's typical of the species, Biff! She **NEVER** tires of gazing adoringly at her own reflection!

tra la la

Hel-LO!

Why is she ALONE, Chip? Don't teen-agers travel in packs?

Not **THIS** teen, Biff! She's an OUTCAST, rejected by her peers! She's what we in the safari biz refer to as... a "LOSER!"

Careful with that dart gun!

I hear you, my friend! There are few things more TER-RIFYING than an angry teen-ager!

POP!
- - - - -

A direct hit! But... OH, **NO!**

The sed-ative isn't working! She's going to charge! **RUN!**

WOO HOO HOO HOO

Peirce

131

bIg NATE

by Lincoln Peirce

MY CAT-LIKE REFLEXES MAKE ME THE **IDEAL** CENTER FIELDER!

THE **INSTANT** I HEAR THE CRACK OF THE BAT, I MOVE! MOVE! **MOVE!**

BE ALERT, NOW... BE READY...

CRACK!

BACK BACK BACK BACK BACK BACK BACK BACK BACK

YES, **REFLEXES!** THE MOST VITAL PART OF BEING A CENTER FIELDER!...

WUMP!

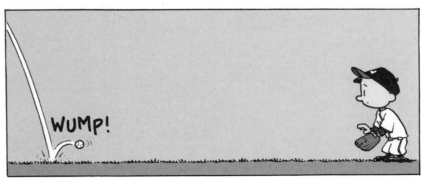

...THOUGH DEPTH PERCEPTION IS KEY, TOO...

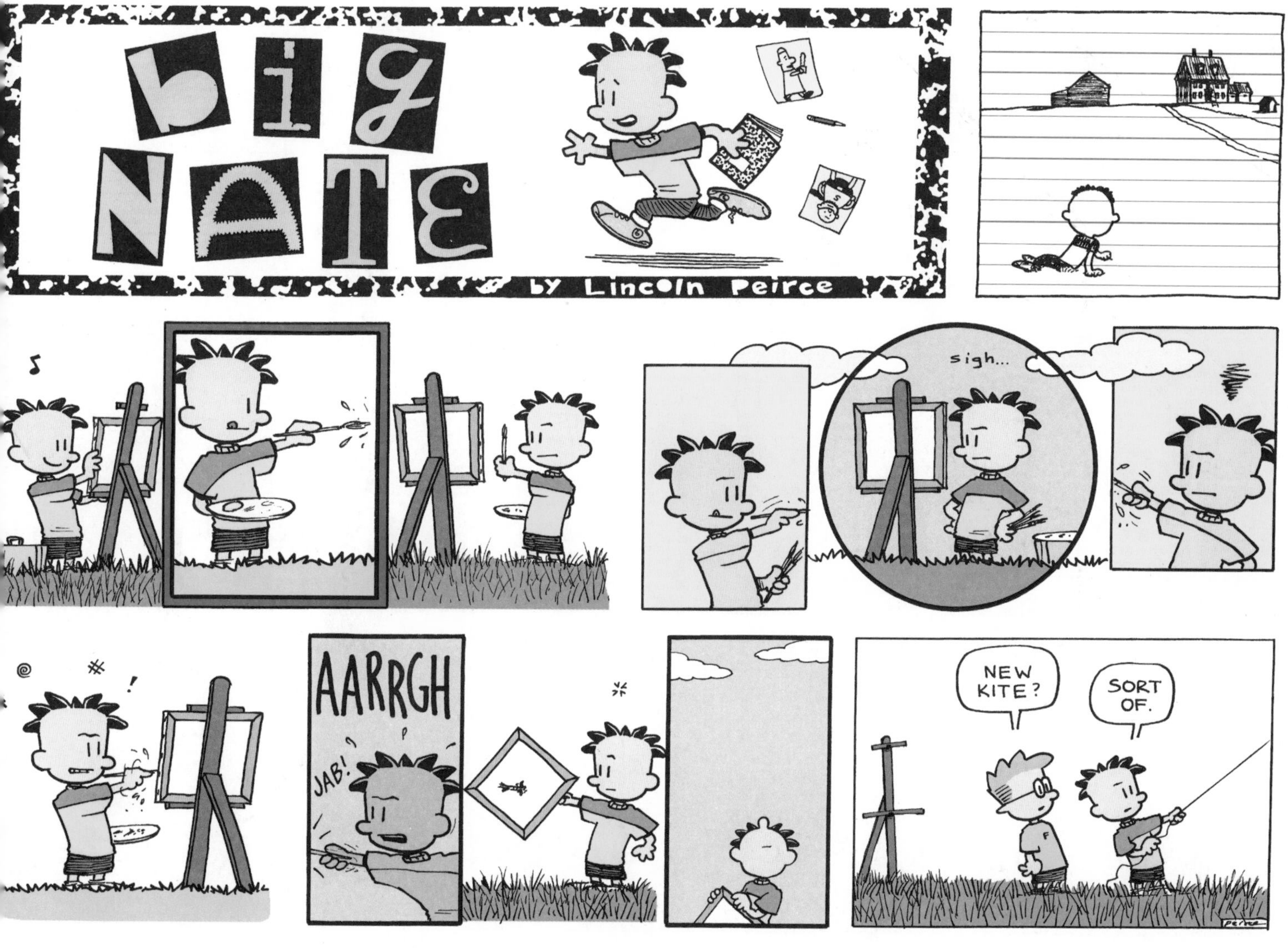
big NATE
by Lincoln Peirce
sigh...
AARRGH
JAB!
NEW KITE?
SORT OF.

DRAWING OF YOUR PET $2.00

OH... HI, MRS. GODFREY.

WELL! DRAWINGS OF PETS! WHAT A GOOD IDEA, NATE!

DRAWING OF YOUR PET $2.00

AND THE PRICE IS RIGHT!

COULD YOU DRAW A PICTURE OF MY BOOTSY?

NO PROBLEMO! WATCH THE MASTER AT WORK!

DRAWING OF YOUR PET $2.00

HUMM DE DUM.... A LINE HERE... HUM HUMM... A LITTLE DARKER OVER THERE... HMM HMM...

VOILA!

WHY, THAT'S VERY GOOD! HOW DID YOU GET IT TO LOOK SO MUCH LIKE HER?

WELL, YOU KNOW HOW PEOPLE LOOK LIKE THEIR PETS?

I JUST DREW A PICTURE OF **YOU**, THEN ADDED SOME EXTRA FACIAL HAIR AND A COLLAR!

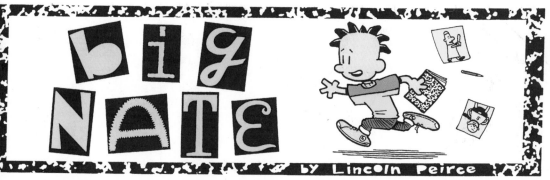
big NATE by Lincoln Peirce

BAM! BAM! BAM!

Time For Another Edition Of...
"WOW! WHAT A MAKEOVER!"

'Allo.

...With *INTERNATIONALLY ACCLAIMED STYLIST*... **MR. PIERRE!**

Friends, today I will be attempting my most challenging makeover EVER: 15-year-old **ELLEN WRIGHT!**

Giggle! Bone joor, Mister Pierre!

Ellen, when I look at you, I clearly see you are a "WINTER" person!

Because I look good in blues and grays?

No, because you should stay indoors.

Let me first apply some "concealer" to your enormous nose...

Sacre bleu! It is not working!

Well then, perhaps I can add some color to your pasty-white, acne-scarred cheeks!

'gad! This makes it WORSE!

...And your coarse, lifeless hair resists even my best conditioner!

Sob! Oh, Mr. Pierre! Can't you help me?

I am sorry, my ugly little duckling. It is beyond even Mr. Pierre's powers.

If you want to change your appearance, you will have to do it on your own, at home.

ANY DAY NOW!

SHUT UP!

by Lincoln Peirce

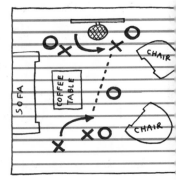

TAP TAP TAP

NATE... — HOLD IT, DAD! I ALREADY KNOW WHAT YOU'RE GOING TO SAY!

YOU DON'T WANT ME HANGING MY HOOP HERE! BUT I'VE GIVEN THIS A LOT OF THOUGHT!

THIS IS THE PERFECT LOCATION! IT'S NOT CLOSE TO ANY FURNITURE! IT'S NOT IN THE WAY OF ANYTHING!

PLUS, FEEL THE BALL! IT'S **FOAM**! IT WON'T BREAK THE LAMPS! IT WON'T CRACK THE PLASTER!

THERE'S ABSOLUTELY NO REASON NOT TO HAVE A HOOP HERE! OKAY, DAD? OKAY?

FINE, NATE. I HAVE NO OBJECTION TO HAVING THE HOOP HERE.

YES!

I WOULD, HOWEVER, LIKE TO DISCUSS THE 3-POINT LINE ON THE KITCHEN FLOOR.

WATCH IT, WATCH IT! THAT'S STILL WET!

bi9 NATE by Lincoln Peirce

STOP THE INSANITY! STOP THE INSANITY!!

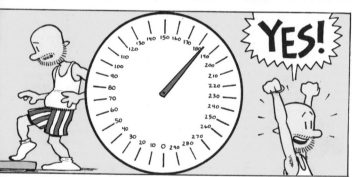

YES!

I **DID** IT! I FINALLY DID IT!

FOR **SIX MONTHS** I'VE BEEN TRYING TO GET MY WEIGHT DOWN UNDER 185!

...AND JUST NOW I **DID** IT! I FINALLY DID IT!!

GREAT JOB, DAD.

PAT PAT

YOU'RE OFFICIALLY OVER THE HILL!

THAT'S "**HUMP**"!!

RIGHT, DAD. KEEP SAYING THAT.

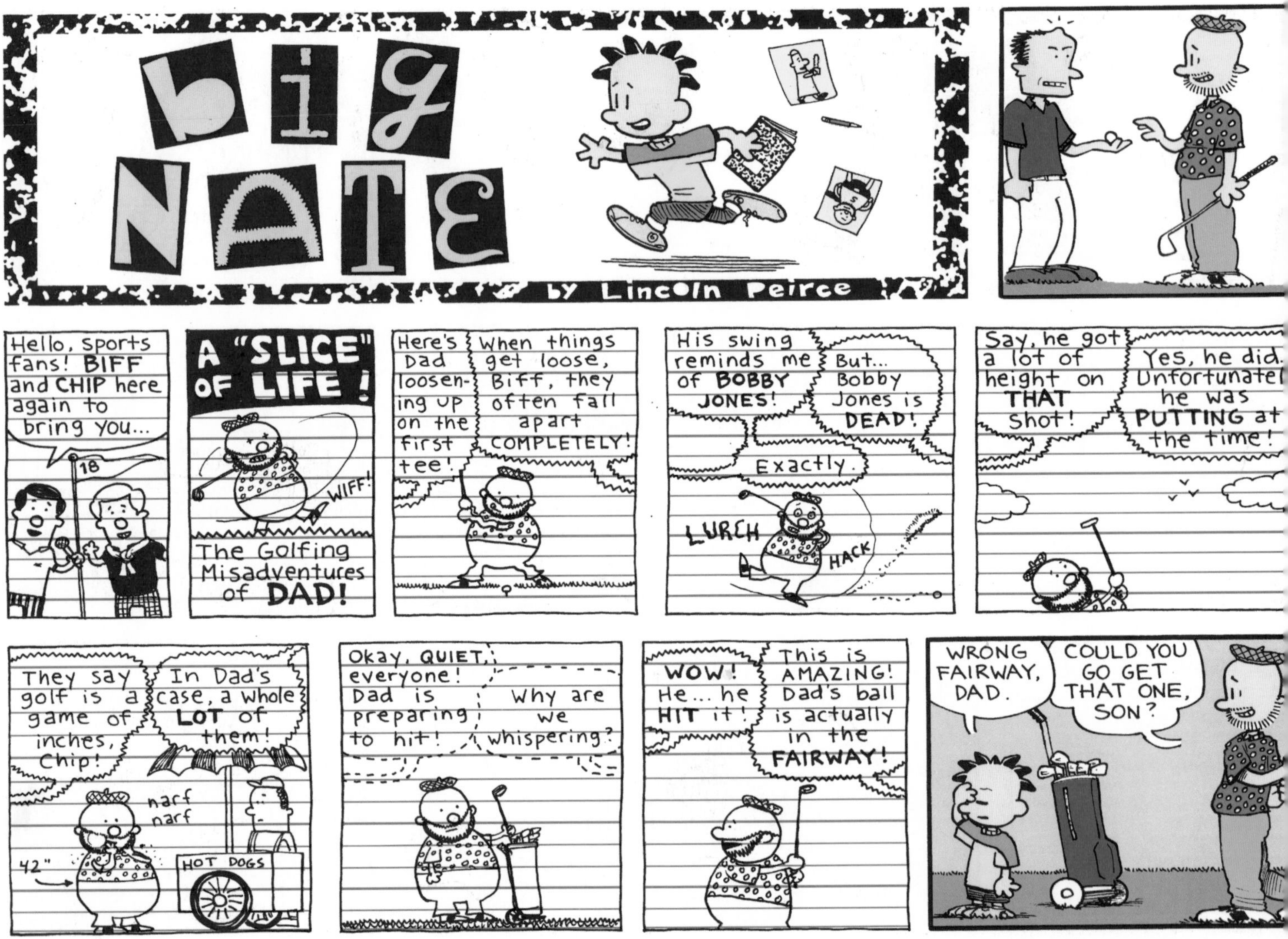
big NATE
by Lincoln Peirce
Hello, sports fans! BIFF and CHIP here again to bring you...
18
A "SLICE" OF LIFE!
WIFF!
The Golfing Misadventures of DAD!
Here's Dad loosening up on the first tee!
When things get loose, Biff, they often fall apart COMPLETELY!
His swing reminds me of BOBBY JONES!
But... Bobby Jones is DEAD!
Exactly.
LURCH
HACK
Say, he got a lot of height on THAT shot!
Yes, he did. Unfortunatel he was PUTTING at the time!
They say golf is a game of inches, Chip!
In Dad's case, a whole LOT of them!
narf narf
42"
HOT DOGS
Okay, QUIET, everyone! Dad is preparing to hit!
Why are we whispering?
WOW! He... he HIT it!
This is AMAZING! Dad's ball is actually in the FAIRWAY!
WRONG FAIRWAY, DAD.
COULD YOU GO GET THAT ONE, SON?

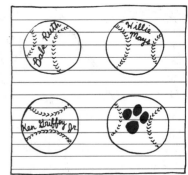

MAN, NOTHING EVER HAPPENS OUT HERE IN RIGHT FIELD!

WOOF!

SPITSY! WHAT ARE YOU DOING HERE, YOU DUMB DOG? SCAT! GO HOME!

NO! DON'T COME ON THE FIELD, YOU IDIOT!

SPITSY! KNOCK IT OFF, YOU FLEABAG! I'M IN THE MIDDLE OF A GAME!

CRACK!

LEGGO, YOU STUPID MUTT! I GOTTA CATCH THE BALL! I GOTTA CATCH THE BALL!

CLOMP!

PTOO!

HI, NATE. IS ELLEN AROUND?

GORDIE! MY MAN! COME ON IN!

ELLEN'S UPSTAIRS. WHILE YOU WAIT, CAN I INTEREST YOU IN A LITTLE LIGHT READING?

LIGHT READING?

YUP! THIS HERE'S A HOT LITTLE PAGE-TURNER ENTITLED "ELLEN'S DIARY"!

LOTS OF GOOD STUFF IN HERE! LIKE **THIS**: "MAY 25TH — THAT MARK KESSLER IS SO **CUTE**! HOPE HE'S MY PARTNER ON THE SCIENCE PROJECT!"

AH! ISN'T THE HONESTY **TOUCHING**? JUST A GIRL, A PEN AND HER DEEPEST, MOST PRIVATE THOUGHTS!

YES, THERE'S NOTHING LIKE A DIARY FOR CHRONICLING ALL THE SIGNIFICANT EVENTS OF —

...CHILDHOOD.

P O W

August 8th — Turning in early. Bad headache.

big NATE

by Lincoln Peirce

"A RAKE'S PROGRESS"

Sigh...

HI, MR. EUSTIS! IT'S THAT TIME OF YEAR AGAIN!

WHAT TIME OF YEAR?

LEAF-RAKING TIME! WANT ME TO DO YOUR LAWN?

NATE, I HIRED YOU TO DO MY LAWN **LAST** YEAR.

...AND AS I RECALL, YOU DIDN'T GET AROUND TO IT UNTIL THERE WAS **SNOW** ON THE GROUND!

THAT WAS AN ORGANIZATIONAL PROBLEM! THAT WON'T HAPPEN **THIS** YEAR!

I'VE GOT A **SYSTEM** NOW! I WRITE EVERY-THING DOWN ON THESE SLIPS OF PAPER!

SEE? NAMES! DATES! I'VE GOT IT ALL RIGHT HERE! THAT WAY, **THIS** YEAR WON'T BE LIKE **LAST** YEAR!

ALL THE YEARS ARE STARTING TO SEEM ALIKE.

by Lincoln Peirce

※SIGH...※

!

FOUND IT!

WANT ME TO LOOK FOR YOUR BALL, TOO?

NO

by Lincoln Peirce

Panel 1: Time once again for the adventures of... **SUPERDAD!**

(the world's **ONLY** bald superhero! with a slight paunch)

Panel 2: And introducing dim-witted sidekick... **MegaTEEN!**

Dang!

She fights crime... **AND** chronic acne!

Panel 3: One fine day...

Ye **GADS!**

What IS it, Super-dad?

Panel 4: It's that fiend **GARBAGE-MAN!** He's coming up the street!

ALREADY? It's not even 8:00 AM!

Panel 5: The devious devil! He **knows** we're not ready for him!

What will we **DO?**

Panel 6: What else?...

dramatic pause

TAKE OUT THE GARBAGE!

Um... what are you looking at **ME** for?

Panel 7: Well, **I** certainly can't do it! Not with my bulging disk!

Well, **I** can't either! Garbage is so smelly and **GROSS!**

Panel 8: Then that means this is a job for...

CHORE-BOY!

Panel 9: **NATE!**